The
REVENANT
OF
Rebecca Pascal

The
REVENANT
of
Rebecca Pascal

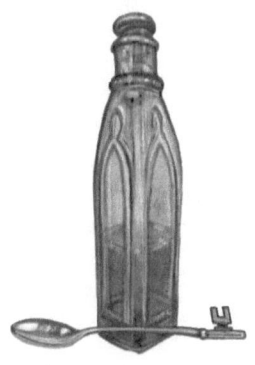

David Barker
& W. H. Pugmire

Weird House Press
Central Point, OR 97502
www.weirdhousepress.com
Join the Weird House mailing list at our website!

Dedication

This book is dedicated to Mike Davis and the *Lovecraft eZine*.

—*D. B. & W.H. P.*

List of Illustrations

PREFACE

Ill-Walked To Arkham

To dream their dreams of Lovecraftian horror …
two set out for Arkham.
Wilum Hopfrog Pugmire
and his boon companion
David Barker.
It was a starless night when they arrived.

Legend-haunted Arkham. Witch-haunted Arkham. Cascades roil in the black ground under certain tombstones in Old Wooded Graveyard. Fell travelers come and go from ill-lit taverns and desolate cafés and blackened doorways where the traveling wind dusts the weary with ancient fragrances.

Stately Arkham.
Crumbling Arkham. Lovecraft's Arkham!

Nonetheless, they went through sunset's gate to encounter many a strange dance only come upon when the great hands of blackness weave uncommon chills. A great hunger gnawing within them, they stood in galleries of apparitions nethescurian and saw (as only poets can see), listened to the poetry (every curse and howl bent by the prisoners of grim and their foulsome keepers), and recorded. Together our poets have stitched together an account of, well … that would be giving away a *very rewarding prize*.

In witch-haunted Arkham they dreamed their softblack Lovecraftian dreams … and in a moment, after you have turned this page and the evening chill holds you in its gnarled hands, you dear reader will enter dreams not unlike many of Georg Trakl's bleak and anguished autumnal sonatas.

Travel carefully … that rustling of dry leaves announces your steps to the things that have removed their rotting mask of flesh and await you in unfriendly rooms.

Joseph S. Pulver, Sr.
Berlin, Germany
January 2014

INTRODUCTION

This novella is one of three books of Lovecraftian fiction that I collaborated on with the late W. H. Pugmire (1951–2019.) It originally wasn't going to be a novella at all; rather we had agreed to write some Lovecraftian short stories together. Toward that end, Wilum had begun a couple of stories, but wasn't happy with them and didn't finish either. When I asked to see them, he said he had thrown away one story but would send me the other. Destroying unfinished drafts was something he did a lot. It always made me cringe to hear about these lost manuscripts. Even a fragment from his rich literary imagination would interest me, and no doubt many of his fans. What he sent me in April 2013 was the beginning of a short story titled "Impressions of the Tomb." At 3,350 words, it had an appealing setting and distinctive characters, but there was no premise or storyline yet.

Wilum proposed that I come up with the basic plot, he would write a rough draft of the full story, and I would revise and polish that. But for some reason, that didn't happen.

What did happen is that I printed out Wilum's story fragment and read it several times, looking for clues as to where he might have been going with it, subliminally if not consciously. At one point, Wilum refers to a character named "Edward Derby"—the protagonist of H. P. Lovecraft's 1933 short story "The Thing on the Doorstep." Considered by many critics to be one of Lovecraft's lesser stories, it's a favorite of mine, and was also one of Wilum's favorites. I love the excessive morbidity of its language and its Gothic imagery, not to mention the intriguing ambiguities concerning the true identity of the minds inhabiting the possessed bodies of key characters in the story. I reread "The Thing on the Doorstep," noting its themes, plot devices, and other specifics that we might adapt for our collaborative story. We weren't setting out to plagiarize HPL or write a fannish rehash of "The Thing on the Doorstep," so much as to create a new, original work that was inspired by and paid tribute to Lovecraft. At the heart of our story would be the time-honored trope of many a horror story: supernatural possession, and the return of a dead person—a "Revenant"—from the grave.

Our collaboration was conducted by email, with me sending Wilum a revised draft of the story with a new scene or two added that extended and expanded his narrative, him coming back with additional scenes of his own, building on what I'd done and adding his own twists and turns, back and forth until the tale grew too long to still be considered a short story or even a novelette and became a novella. This development was a happy surprise to us, as we were merely hoping to create a decent short story. After seven months of writing, *The Revenant of Rebecca Pascal* was completed in November 2013 and published by Joe Morey's Dark Renaissance Books in 2014. Now, eight years later, the book is being reprinted by Joe's new imprint, Weird House Books.

Working with Wilum was a real joy. His prose was so richly sensuous, the scenes he painted so haunting, his language so evocative, that I was invariably inspired to write my best, striving to attain the level of literary quality that he had set. Wilum's intense, vivid prose stimulated my own creativity. His characters became my characters. I got into their heads, thought their thoughts, experienced their feelings. I even dreamed about them—whole scenes in character that I incorporated into my parts of the narrative. Wilum and I were on the same wavelength while writing this book. Rereading it now, I often can't tell who wrote what. Our literary instincts complemented one another, in that we both leaned towards Gothic themes and a formality of prose style such as one finds in classic horror fiction, rather than the more pared down, conversational style used by most modern horror authors.

Almost a decade later, I'm still very happy with this book. The characters feel quite real to me, like old friends and acquaintances, and the setting feels almost like home. The moral and spiritual ambiguity of the resurrected Rebecca, who genuinely loves her grandnephew, Richard, on the one hand, while ruthlessly advancing the evil designs of the malignant supernatural entity Kamog on the other, endlessly fascinates me. And Richard's apparent naivety regarding Rebecca's true nature—his blindness regarding discrepancies between what she says versus what she does—equally intrigues me. This is a story I can truly live in. I hope it has the same effect on its readers, now and for many years to come.

David Barker

CHAPTER ONE

I wandered through the north side of Arkham, through a fine mist that was neither fog nor rain, along West Armitage Street, until coming at last to the Desolate Café. The site was famous among students attending Miskatonic University, for it was during the café's earliest years that such notorious poets as Justin Geoffrey and Arkham's doomed Edward Derby had declaimed their work there. Once a hangout for high-class bohemians and students who had money, the place had deteriorated over the decades, as had its bill of fare and clientele; yet it remained a gathering place for strange poetic souls, and my great-aunt was known to have recited there, which gave the place a personal touch that I appreciated. Sitting at a table near the platform that served as stage, I ordered coffee and corn chowder, and then I studied that evening's crowd. There were the usual number of college students, and at one table I recognized the notorious members of an Arkham witch cult. I also noted some rather ancient faces, patrons who had spent many decades in the mellow light of the place; and in one corner I caught sight of a slouched figure who mumbled to the shadows that crowded her corner of the establishment. I thought, at times, that she was scrutinizing me as I bent over my bowl and devoured my repast; and once I was certain that she winked at me wickedly. She laughed at nothing as I turned my attention from her and finished my meal, and I looked at her boldly when I rose to take my soup bowl and coffee cup to the tub where customers dropped off their plates and such. I could not discern her age through the filth in which her face was sheathed.

I approached the rows of chairs that had been set up before a podium and sat at the end of one row with some few of the poets whom I recognized from previous readings. The atmosphere was one I relished, one that was rare in my nondescript existence. I can't quite explain it, but to love poetry, to be a poet today, is to feel apart from the clamorous modern world. Everyone around me, in daily life, seems so loud and frantic, fleeing here and there, involved with what I see as life's trivialities. Poetry is a quiet, contemplative realm, a solace from the hectic world of humanity. Giles, one of the two gay men who owned the establishment, approached the podium and began the evening's reading with a sonnet by Dante. Some few other attendees who had been ordering coffee sat behind me, and we grew silent and appreciative as patrons rose and read or recited. The poetry that evening was pleasant but not remarkable—until the weird woman I had noticed earlier waddled to the podium, brushing against my sleeve as she passed my chair. I took in her earthy odor—not an unpleasant "homeless" smell, although she looked like a denizen of gutters and alleys. She stood before us, nodding and grinning as she unfolded a stained sheet of paper; then she began to speak, in a voice that was inexpressibly beautiful.

> "You come to us from beyond the other side,
> beyond midnight and moonlight, seeping
> toward us as a stain, a blot, a pool.
> I lift my silver slipper from the sod,
> my silver slipper stained with mud and straw,
> but cannot step into the air, to you.
> Fall to earth, claw into the sod, wash with filth and clay.

2

Face me with your potency and call my name.
There—there, that effluvium, that breath of deity
that encases me. Once more I stand, your Eve,
your Golem, molded by your alchemy.
How is it that, attired in these elements of earth,
I am a weightless thing? Your air, your liquid
exhalation, beckons my new-formed limbs.
I lift my sodden slipper, my slipper stained
with mud and straw, and step into your soul,
to your essence that is now my territory."

Her effect on me was hypnotic, and as she spoke I forgot about her discolored teeth, the disarray of her tattered clothing, her unwashed face and matted hair. When, abruptly, she ceased speaking and crept to huddle again in her corner, I wanted to protest. Her words had woven impressions in my brain; I felt possessed by half-glimpsed things, phantoms that I ached to understand. I was so mentally preoccupied with her effect on my psyche that I couldn't listen to the others who recited, and a sudden need for air pushed me from my chair and out the door. I scanned the blackness of night, seeing it as never before, and felt a little foolish as I lifted my foot as if some sorcery would allow me to step into the air, an attempt that was met with a rising wind, chill and remorseless, that kissed my ear with strange sighs as it froze my flesh. Then I heard another breathing, and I turned to face the poet in her drab attire. She lifted an unlit cigarette.

"Got a match?"

"Sorry, no. I don't smoke."

She shrugged. "Don't be sorry. I'll enjoy it another day." Pocketing the noxious weed, she examined the sky. "Well, the mist is gone. Rather warm tonight." I laughed at this and shivered again. Perhaps if I had been homeless, such a night wouldn't seem so cold compared to others. Squinting at me she said, "You don't look so well. Go back in and have a cup of hot tea."

I shook my head. "No, it's just the chilliness of the wind."

"Ain't no wind tonight."

I opened my mouth to protest, but then the world grew silent and I realized that she was right. "This is insanely weird," I muttered to myself. "What was that incantation that you spoke in there, from what secret book did you cull it? Yes, those weird words; I can still feel them in my brain, like wet clinging leaves." Stupidly, I laughed. "I've heard of Arkham witchery, but this is my first true encounter with it. You look the role as well, with your shabby clothes and pungent smell of—age. Is that what that odor is, that earthly bouquet? It's as if dirt has been packed into your pores."

She laughed at me and winked. "Nar, that's the smell o' me bed."

Her reply seemed playful, as though she had an amusing secret and was laughing at me. I could not comprehend the creature, and confusion blossomed into anger. Her eyes studied mine and I saw her expression darken. Her stance grew erect, and when she spoke again it was with the musical voice with which she had recited inside the café.

"I lie in the earth, among the souls at rest,
among the souls who do not rest. We hearken
to movements in tall grasses, to motion beneath
tall grasses, to sounds beneath the crust within
a maze of tunnels secret and unseen.
'Secret.' How oft we use that word
to describe this witch-town and its ways.
Ah, the secret ways will not be rushed,
are now but rarely noticed, however regular

4

their waves. They care not for the busy world
of brutes. No, they coax the dreamer, the sensitive soul.
Did you know that modernity has corrupted dreaming?
The facile crowd dream only of their little lives,
their insubstantial time. They fear to feel
the waves of witchery. But this is Arkham,
and towns can dream of their pregnant past
and recollect the bygone ways. The secret ways.
Oh, the rare dreams I have tasted, in my shallow pit
of sod, my fragrant bed beneath the stars."

Although I experienced an inner chill at the sound of her
voice and queer language, I grinned and looked away from her,
to the sky. "Well, you'll see no stars tonight. There's nothing up
there but utter darkness."

Raising a soiled hand, she pointed a crooked finger to the
sky. "There," she whispered. My eyes looked to where she was
pointing, and I saw a dim, distant spark that gradually grew
brighter. One brilliant star shimmered in the blackness above us.
Astounded, I turned to regard her, only to find that she was gone.
Then I noticed the vague silhouette some way from me, and crept
after it, following with no concern for time or place, as if I were
trailing some phantom in a dream. It seemed that I had followed
her forever when, at last, she entered a fenced-off burying ground.
I stepped into the place and walked through tall grass past tilting
timeworn tombstones. She led me past stones and tall pillars, to
an enormous ancient yew tree that spread its sinister branches
over ground and graves. Completely ignoring me, the creature
knelt at a spot that was void of grass or shrub, next to a shallow
indentation in the earth around which a pattern made of twigs
and leaves had been placed.

"What did they name ye?"

… I had followed her forever when, at last, she entered a fenced-off burying ground.

The sudden sound of her voice, her revealed awareness of my presence, startled me. "I'm Richard Pascal."

My reply made her shudder, and she turned to face me with astonished eyes. I watched, as she drifted to me, as she leaned close and studied my face. "I see it now, Rebecca's eyes and nose. You're the lad from Chicago who inherited her house. We've been curious about you."

"We?"

Strangely, she raised her hands above her head, began to hum a silly tune, and danced toward the tree. I watched her bend to the ground and find a small wooden box which she lifted and showed me. "She used to recite at the café, years ago. Never seen any of her films, but I saw her dancing on this ground once, in moonlight."

Opening the container's lid, she took out a photograph and offered it to me. I went to her and took the photo as she hummed in a low tone. The photo was a publicity pose from one of Rebecca's films of the 1940s. The creature's low humming became a sigh of words. "Yes, you resemble her, in your clumsy masculine way."

I sensed a movement of distant shadows. Something howled to night tide. "What is this place?"

"Hangman's Hill. The Miskatonic is yonder—it calls to me sometimes, when I'm sleeping."

"I've never been in this section of town. Damn, it's dark here. I can't see any street lamps. Isn't this place supposed to be dangerous? I read somewhere of a corpse being found at Old Wooded Graveyard."

She shrugged. "Bodies are found. It is especially dark, isn't it?" Something in her tone unnerved me, and I thought she was playing at spooking me. "There's a road just there; you can get to it by climbing over the fence. Bus to town'll be here soon enough. It'll take you to the light."

7

Her performance was effective, and a feeling of curious fear came over me. Abruptly, I turned and fled, rushed to the dilapidated iron fence and climbed over it. Too nervous to wait for a bus, I marched along the street, to town, disturbed at one point when I began to whistle a tune I did not know, but then recognized as the melody that the strange woman had been humming. I entered town and hailed a taxi to my aunt's house on top of Frenchman's Hill. Once home, I didn't turn on any lights, but slipped into the spacious library and lit one solitary candle, the glow of which dimly illuminated a large framed portrait of my great-aunt, the film actress and poet Rebecca Pascal.

I had visited her some few times, as a child, when my mother took me to Arkham for a visit lasting one or two weeks. I cherished those visits as a lad, for my aunt was like no one I had ever encountered, then or since. She had flair, she bubbled over with gaiety, she was famous. I loved those rare special nights when she would perform for us, reciting speeches from her films or poetry she had penned. Yet as I matured, we grew distant. I had a feeling that my dull life would intrude upon what I suspected was her glamorous existence, and so I forgot her and settled into a drab routine. She never wrote, except for a card when my mother unexpectedly passed away from cancer. Shortly afterward came the news of my great-aunt's death, and the astounding revelation that I had inherited her house in Arkham and her fortune.

I was fifty-three years of age and tired of my humdrum life, and the idea of using my newly obtained two million dollars to build a new existence for myself in Arkham was greatly appealing. My passion was for reading, and my aunt had collected a magnificent library that would serve me well for my remaining days. I was happy for some few months, existing in a reclusive life of silence and solitude, surrounded by beautiful antiques, eating in excellent restaurants, sleeping in a comfortable bed. But then I became restless—life was *too* cozy and quiet, solitude turned to loneliness. I was not clever enough to keep myself entertained; reading day after day became a bore. In my other life I had sometimes ventured out to a local dive where city poets gathered so as to sip coffee and read their unpublished works. Asking about in the places where I dined, I discovered that a popular café held weekly poetry readings, and so I began to attend these. I wasn't a poet myself, but I took Aunt Rebecca's book and read from it. Thus I discovered how potent a legend my aunt was, and before I knew it, a journalist had asked to interview me at home.

The article and accompanying photograph of me standing below my great-aunt's large portrait gave me a local interest, although people respected my privacy, which they compared to the behavior of my aunt, whom no one disturbed unless invited. One little thing about my sudden notoriety annoyed me, however, and that was when people asked me what I "did." I sensed a kind of disapproval in their faces when I answered that I did nothing except exist. It was then that I got the idea of writing a biography of my aunt, a project on which I planned to linger for a few years. Writing such a book would give me an occupation and aid my social needs, such as they were. I was unable to locate any correspondence written by my aunt to aid my research into her life, but I did find three large diaries in which she recorded her mild success as a film actress. One pleasing aspect of my project was that I encountered a number of people in town who had memories of my aunt and shared those recollections with me.

One change was noticeable after I had lived in my aunt's house for a while—I began to dream vividly. I had never paid much attention to my dreams before arriving in Arkham, for they were mostly confused episodes related to my work life as dish washer and prep cook, scenes of stress in which I wasn't able to function properly in my work environment. This changed, radically, when I settled into my aunt's house and began to study her life. Suddenly, I began to dream of her—or, rather, as her, for I would reenact scenes from her life that had been revealed from reading her private journals; or I would find myself in scenes from her films, films that she had collected on video tape and that I watched as I prepared to record her biography. The most vivid dreams all took place in Arkham, in her home, among a select circle of poets and aesthetes with whom she commingled. One recurring dream intrigued me keenly, for I recognized the scene as that of the Old Wooded Graveyard to which I had been led by the homeless poet. In those dreams, I would see my aunt, dressed in flowing white and looking like a spectre, drifting over the graveyard as she held something with both hands, something that she pressed to her breast. My aunt would float to one spot in the cemetery and kneel on the ground, setting her object beside her as she dug into the earth. Satisfied with her labor, she would slide the object into the hole and begin to nod. The camera of my dream would move in for a close-up on my aunt's shadowed face, the eyes of which would suddenly rise to peer directly at me. I felt myself being pulled into those eyes, and I would feel my flesh grow numb with fear. Then I would awaken. But the last time I experienced this dream, it did not end thus; and as I studied her face it seemed more youthful than before. The scene was in semi-darkness until, above us, clouds moved away from the moon. I watched, and my great-aunt's eyes turned black and liquid as the flesh of her visage distorted with hoary age. I watched, as her awful hands lifted and clutched at her distorting countenance, as she removed the rotting mask of flesh from her skull and dropped it into the earthen pit.

CHAPTER TWO

I turned my face to morning light. I had chosen the smallest of the upper guest rooms as my bedroom, preferring it to the more spacious boudoirs with their fancy furnishings. The room was simplicity itself, and yet still touched by my great-aunt's eccentricities. I somehow related to its neglected aspect, for I often felt like an abandoned soul. Much as I loved my independence, I was lonely. Living alone in such a huge house seemed to accentuate my sense of isolation. This new life felt odd and a bit overwhelming, and the idea came to me that I might be better off selling the house and auctioning off its fabulous contents. Yet I was lazy and complacent, and it would take more determination than I possessed to do anything so radical and demanding. So much easier just to accept my fate, to grow old in this venerable abode. I was no longer youthful, and I was not ambitious.

I stretched and shut my eyes, not ready to leave the warmth of my bedclothes. Then hunger gnawed, and not being fond of cooking, I dressed and drove to a small café that served an excellent breakfast menu at all hours. Their eggs Benedict was excellent, washed down with a glass of orange juice. Halfway through my repast I heard the doorbell tinkle as someone entered, and cold air brushed me momentarily. Someone called my name, and I glanced up at the portly fellow who regarded me. "Mr. Lorne, good morning."

"Good afternoon, you mean. Do call me Wilus. May I join you? May I order you a latté? Are you still interested in showing me your aunt's library? She must have some fabulously rare items!"

Having sat, he leaned his black cane against his leg and raised a hand. "Brenda, darling, two almond lattés, and I'll have a buttered poppy-seed scone, slightly heated. Thank you, dear." I watched as he shut his eyes and tilted his egg-shaped head, and then listened to the cracking of his neck bones.

Opening his eyes, he regarded me somberly. "Oh dear, you're looking annoyed. Am I clutching at you? But you did invite me to look at your library, two weeks ago at the poetry reading. You remember how attracted I was to your personal copy of your aunt's poems, and then you mentioned, nonchalantly, that you had found a small box with more copies of that rare item. Well! She wasn't a great poet—her greatness was reserved for her film acting, and there she was superb!—but she had a certain flair, and she wrote so intriguingly about this town and its secrets. How could I not be *fascinated?*"

Reaching into an ample pocket, Lorne produced a small yellow book. "This is my finest collection of vignettes and prose poems. I want you to have a copy. I have inscribed it to you, in ink of lilac hue. Will you accept this gift? My work is inspired in part by your aunt's book and will facilitate your curiosity regarding the history of Arkham, which you mentioned the other night when you spoke of writing a book about Rebecca. She was rooted to this old locale in ways you cannot guess. I knew her slightly, yet in a secret way that she did not reveal to many. Oh, the things I can whisper to you!"

Our coffees and his scone arrived. I sipped mine and nodded. "This coffee is good. Facts or legends?"

"Hmmm?"

"The things you could whisper to me."

Oh, his sly smile. "A delicious serving of both, dear boy. Her life as she half-revealed it to our community, and her life as it was touched by Outside influence."

"What's that?"

"Surely you've felt it. One can hardly escape it here in Arkham, it's in the air we breathe. It's a kind of 'knowing' that comes to us when we are alone in shadowy places, and it sometimes taints our dreams. It's a sixth sense by which we are plugged into what is often called the occult. Some few become intimate with it, and they are sometimes called witches or sorcerers—or lunatics. Your aunt was such a one. She owned a special library of books that served as psychic paths to hidden ways and realms. Let me help you find those books." His eyes became slits and he tilted his head a little. "You *did* invite me, Richard."

I could see he wasn't going to let up. Although I found him an interesting, if somewhat absurd, character, there was an element of greediness in him that I found off-putting. He seemed to sense my disdain and changed tactics.

"You must find me demanding for one you only just met. Have I been rude, Richard? I am keenly fascinated with your aunt and her history, with that house that you have inherited and its legend. But I have a professional interest as well. You see, I'm a book scout, always on the hunt for rare items. I'm connected to a lot of people who pay good prices for rare titles. I believe your aunt owned some rather fabulous books that could bring us both quite a lot of money, if you'd be willing to part with them. I'm extremely good at what I do. I combine my business acumen with my bibliographic passion. I do get carried away, however, and I judge from your coolness that I have offended you."

"No, not at all," I countered. "I'm not a social person, that's all, especially at home. Why not come over tomorrow night, around seven?"

"Excellent! I'll bring my checkbook. Oops, there I go again, too animated! I cannot help myself. I've passed by your aunt's house so many times over the years, wondering at its fate, remembering my few times inside it. Every time I pass it I can almost feel Rebecca's presence lingering there, her so potent personality. Do you believe in such things, that a person's personality may linger and be left in some component in the places where she lived?"

"I've felt her there, certainly, but I'm surrounded by the things she owned, by the style with which she decorated her home, and, too, I've been watching the videos of her old films. Well, come tomorrow night, and we shall toast her memory and invade her library. I'll see you then."

I sipped the last of my coffee and prepared to depart when our attention was drawn to a minor clamor coming from the direction of the front entrance. The homeless female poet I had followed the other night was standing just inside the door, casting a weird eye about the establishment. I suspected that she was hoping for a free meal from some kind soul, or at least a cup of coffee. Spotting me, her eyes lit up dramatically and she rushed to our table, her filthy rags brushing against some of the other seated patrons.

"Oh, dear," Lorne whispered, "it's Julia in all her filth."

"You know her?"

He nodded. "One of Arkham's most promising young poets—twenty years ago. *Julia*, darling, what a dramatic entrance! You're looking well."

She looked anything but well. Standing there in her dirty rags, as disheveled as any common vagrant, I was struck by how different this Julia seemed, compared to the person who had declaimed poetry to a crowd. Then she had infected me with her exotic language and the beauty of her voice. The creature before us now possessed none of that power; she was void of gorgeous strangeness, nothing other than a desperate guttersnipe.

"Do you gents mind if I sit here with you?"

"You're about to be ejected, I'm afraid. Let's go sit outside.

Wilus, will you order another coffee for our friend?" Standing, I offered the woman my hand, and after a moment's hesitation she took it and walked with me to one of the tables outdoors. The air was cool but not unpleasant. Lorne soon joined us, with two new cups of the delicious coffee.

"I've ordered you a breakfast sandwich, my dear. I hope you like ham. I cannot stay myself, and Mr. Pascal and I have finished our business. Oh, I've left my cane hanging on my chair inside. Ta, darlings!"

She said nothing and did not watch him as he left us, giving her full attention to the coffee cup, holding it in both hands as if it were some sacred relic. When her sandwich arrived she gobbled one half of it, and then pushed the plate aside and leaned back into her chair, sighing as if she had unloaded some heavy burden. I waited for her to speak, but she seemed disinclined to do so.

"You made quite an impression on me the other night, Julia."

"Eh? Oh, my reading. Yes. Had one of my episodes. They come when I recite sometimes."

"Episodes."

"When I become possessed. When the words spoken ain't my own. When I'm taken over. Don't look at me like that. It's exhilarating when it happens. It's what I feel when I'm writing poetry, a fantastic sensation, stuff pours out that I could never write in a 'normal' state of mind. Sure, I could compose a poem for you right here on the spot, and it would be pretty good, probably. It would have craft. But it wouldn't be alive like those I write when *she* takes over."

"She? You mean your Muse?"

"She's that, I guess. I, um, hesitate to tell you more, it's kind of awkward. Best I keep it to myself."

"I enjoy awkwardness, Julia. I can't pretend to understand this thing that happens to you, not that it's any of my business. It has nothing to do with me personally."

15

God, what a *queer* look she gave me! She began to eat the other half of her breakfast sandwich, and the rest of our conversation was not terribly noteworthy. Julia complained of the aches and pains she suffered, and I lamented the boredom that had me in its clutches since moving to my aunt's house. Finally, I rose to leave, knowing there would be no more talk of her bizarre behavior the night of the reading. I wanted to ask why it was she slept in the graveyard, in the dirt and among the tombstones, but I refrained. Somehow, however, she seemed to read my mind.

"She's buried there, you know? She worked it somehow, when she was young, to buy one final lot on a small incline over where the rich people rot, even though there hadn't been burials there for decades."

"Yes, I've seen photos of it."

"But you haven't visited her yet." She looked at me so strangely, and then, suddenly, she rushed away. No, I had not visited my aunt's tomb. For some reason, the idea of doing so depressed me acutely.

CHAPTER THREE

The following evening a little after seven o'clock, Lorne rang my doorbell. He brought with him a bottle of decent California wine, a house-warming gift. "Something to get us in the mood for poring over antique volumes," he explained.

I thanked him, opened it, and poured us both a glass, although I intended on having no more than one or two sips. I needed to remain clear-headed for any dealings with him.

We moved from the parlor into the library with our glasses and he leaned his black cane against a chair as he sighed in admiration of the room, its fine rosewood paneling, its magnificent carved mantelpiece, the built-in shelves lining the walls and neatly packed with hundreds of vintage books. The boxful of copies of my great-aunt's book of poems sat on a long work table. I took out a handful and laid them before him, and Lorne picked up one, opened it and read from its title page.

"Ah," he said, flipping back to the front free endpaper where Rebecca had scribbled her name in flowing blue ink, "this copy is signed."

"They all are. She signed them pretty much the same way, with her name and the date."

He nodded happily. "Collectors love signed material. Makes it easier to sell, and for a better price. How many copies are here?"

"Twenty-two copies, but only half of those are for sale. I want to keep the rest for handing out to poets I meet at the Desolate Café."

"Fair enough." He seemed disappointed, having already done the math on his profits from twenty-two copies, but he didn't press for a larger share of them. We agreed on a price that I felt was modest but sufficient. I didn't need the money, and mainly I wanted more space in the library for the boxes of my own books. Lorne asked if there were any other books I'd be willing to sell. There were. My aunt had accumulated perhaps one hundred volumes of the history of World War One, a subject in which I had no interest, and I wanted to unload them. Lorne wasn't greatly thrilled by these but saw the potential for a modest profit if he sold the lot on eBay. He offered me a flat two dollars per volume.

"Make that three dollars and you've got a deal," I said, playing at driving a hard bargain. It was still a good price, and he accepted.

I assumed he would pack up and leave at this point but he kept looking around the room as if he were searching for something in particular. "Did your aunt have, by any chance, anything on the occult arts—magic, witchcraft, sorcery, and the like?"

"No, nothing like that."

"You're certain?"

"I've looked through most of the books in this room and not found anything in that category. I would have remembered it if I had. I don't think she owned any books of that persuasion."

Lorne didn't seem to want to believe me. I don't know if he thought I was lying, or hiding such books from him, or simply ignorant of my aunt's holdings. "That's odd, because I happen to know she consulted such works often during the period when I was an admittedly minor member of her circle, and I've heard rumors that she had, in fact, a sizable library on the occult."

I shrugged. "Not that I know of. If she did, she must have sold it all before her death. Look all you like: there's nothing resembling such titles in this room." What I didn't mention was that I hadn't conducted a thorough search of the entire contents of the house. The fact was, there were books everywhere, in many bedrooms, in antique cabinets, tucked away in closets, filling trunks in the attic and basement. Rebecca had been a book hoarder and had them squirreled away in every available space. I lacked the energy and interest to go through it all in a systematic way. Now and then I would happen across one of her innumerable books, pick it up and read a few pages, and then stuff it back where I found it; but I made no effort to examine, organize, or catalog the countless titles. She may very well have had books on the Black Arts. I hadn't yet come across any, and if I had I would not have let Lorne see them, let alone purchase any. The idea of this rotund freak probing into my aunt's private proclivities was abhorrent to me. If she dabbled in such uncouth matters, I would suppress that fact from anyone outside the immediate family.

"Well, that's strange. You should surely investigate that aspect of her life in your biography! Family skeletons are such a bore."

I felt a chill pass through me, for he seemed to have read my mind. I remained silent as he wrote me a check, and then I helped him lug his purchases to the minivan parked in front of the house, with him carrying one large box under his arm as his other hand grasped his walking stick. He had a slight limp, and so I supposed that the cane was more than affectation. Muttering his goodbyes, he climbed into his vehicle and drove off.

For the rest of the evening, I felt disturbed, even anxious. Lorne's insistence about the existence of my aunt's alleged paranormal library had an unsettling effect upon my mind. Admittedly, I had only been a small child the few times I was around her and obviously as such was not privy to any unpleasant information concerning her that might have discouraged my mother from allowing me to be near Rebecca and her ways.

My aunt had always been kind to me, dependably loving in her somewhat distant, reserved manner that was characteristic of my grandparent's generation, and always seemed far too preoccupied with the minutiae of tending the slowly fading glory of her film stardom to have had the time or energy to invest in any foolish and irresponsible dabbling in magick. I did not—and could not—believe there was any substance to the rumors of her "secret" library that Lorne had cited; and yet, the possibility that such a thing existed cast an uneasy shadow over the rest of the evening, one I was not sure would dissipate after a good night's slumber.

Unable to focus on the evening's reading, I decided to retire earlier than usual. I had experimented with sleeping in various rooms in the large house, but hesitated when I came to one remembered door. This had been the small bedroom where I had slept when visiting my aunt as a child, and I remembered that the bed was very comfortable indeed; yet there was something about the shadows in the room that had disquieted the wee me, and I would sometimes sing nursery songs so as to calm my subtle sense of fear. On one troubled night, the door to the room opened and my aunt entered and sat upon the bed. I liked the warmth and pressure of her body pressed against my blanketed form. She smiled, and moved her head in time to my warbling, and then her lips parted in accompaniment. Finally our song ended, and she reached to smooth her hand through my hair.

"The shadows are scary," I whispered to her.

Oh, her magical smile. She took up the matchbook on the bedside table and lit one candle. "I love the shadows," she said in a low and musical voice. "I love how they frolic, so carefree, in the corners and melt into each other; then they take on fantastic forms such as you have never seen; and sometimes they draw curiously near, and you feel that if you reach out to touch them they might feel like midnight silk."

"They're scary," I reminded her.

She pointed a finger to the ceiling. "I have a remedy for that." Winking, as if about to share some secret, she reached into a pocket and produced a slim green bottle. The candlelight shimmered queerly in her magnetic eyes as she shook the bottle and placed it on the stand. Reaching again into the pocket of her gown, she brought out a small and curiously ornate silver spoon, the handle of which ended in a kind of key. "Silver is one of the colors of dreaming, did you know that?" I shook my head. Rebecca pointed at the bottle with one slender finger. "That is a wonderful potion, a very mild mixture of wormwood and Eastern spices. But it doesn't work unless you sip it from this magick spoon. And ... you have to *really desire* it, as you crave holidays and apples. I'll let you try it—but only if you *really* want to."

"Yes, please."

My aunt bent to reach for the bottle, and I was aware of her scent, which always filled me with delight. She smelt of warmth and womanhood and something that my little brain couldn't quite define. I watched as she unclasped the small bottle and poured some of its fragrant liquid into the spoon. I watched as she brought the spoon to her lips and sipped. Shutting her eyes, she purred, and then she offered the spoon to me. The elixir tasted a little like licorice, but with a more potent flavor, and it felt warm as it slipped down my throat. My aunt's hand played with my hair; her mouth was at my ear; then her mouth slipped to my own, and her fingers tightened at my scalp as the fingers of her other hand pinched out the candle's flame.

Memory melted away. Quietly, I turned the doorknob and pushed. The bed was larger than I remembered it. A window had been left open, and moonlight faintly illuminated the bedchamber as a gentle wind moved long lace curtains. I watched the shadows for a little while, and then moved into the room and sat on the bed. Glancing at the bedside table, I saw a candle in its holder. I saw the small green bottle and silver spoon. How weird, to feel that I was already dreaming and sensing that in dream I could do any audacious thing and still be "safe," although safe from what, I could not fathom. I considered lighting the candle but decided against it, not wanting to distract from the ghostly effects of moonlight and shadow. Picking up the silver spoon with my sinister hand, I tapped its cool surface against my face, just above my left eye. The bottle, when I wrapped fingers around it, was also chilly, and so light that I feared its contents had completely evaporated over the years. I twisted its cap and tipped its opening over the spoon, and then watched the pale green liqueur spill into the shallow bowl. The spoon floated to my mouth and I sipped; then, replacing the things I held on the bedside stand, I lifted my legs onto the bed and leaned my torso against the oak bed board. As I listened to the night, the wind increased in force and moaned a remembered lullaby from childhood. Shutting eyes, I hummed in accompaniment, as darkness and candlelight frolicked on my eyelids. Opening my eyes just a fraction, I watched the shadows that moved through moonbeams. One coil of darkness separated from the other gloom and twisted toward me, and as I closed my eyes again I could feel the pressure of a thing that stroked my hair. Chilliness pressed against my forehead, my cheek, my mouth. Something echoed the wind's lullaby at my ear, and I hummed softly.

I fell into dreaming, into a vision so intimate and vivid that it seemed a different manner of psychic phenomenon than the weird dreams I'd been having of late. Like those, this dream took place in my great-aunt's house, but not in the present day. It was set many years ago, in the days when I had been a child, but in the dream I was a grown adult, one among a crowd of others who were assembled for some special event hosted by Aunt Rebecca. She was young and full of vitality, as beautiful as she appeared on screen. I and a few other late arrivals were ushered into a room where a meeting or celebration of some sort was in progress. It was a room with which I was unfamiliar, and I was startled at this room's very existence, for I thought I had investigated most of the rooms during my months of residence. The way we entered this previously unknown chamber was by walking through one of the lavishly outfitted bedrooms upstairs and then passing through a long, narrow closet to a secret door. The doorway, small and low, opened onto a cramped space that was quite rough and plain in nature compared to the rest of the house. There were chairs placed around the periphery of the room with people seated in them. Aunt Rebecca stood in the center, reading from an open book in a sultry, incantatory tone of voice. Affixed to the walls behind the chairs were primitive bookcases of unfinished lumber, built haphazardly, as if they had been thrown together in haste by some intoxicated carpenter. These cases were burdened with old books in great profusion, with more books stacked horizontally on top of each row of books, and still more volumes piled on the floor between chairs and cases. I glanced at a few titles and was struck with a sudden reeling dizziness. At first I thought that I had become ill, but after a moment I realized it was mortal panic—not sickness—affecting me, and I began to hyperventilate as I recognized the nature of the volumes—their awful and unholy quiddity. These were banned books of the most pernicious kind, vile antique tomes whose very titles have gained an offensive celebrity by having been mentioned in the writings of some of our most distinguished authors of supernatural fiction.

I stood there, aghast and unable to move, as my aunt looked up from her book and locked her eyes onto mine. Her nature changed as she seemed to shift from human into something wild and bestial. A feral look took over her face, and her voice deepened and grew raspy. Yet she continued her reading, although her language was unintelligible. I wanted to flee, to run from the room and escape the house; but I could not break away—she held me in her stare. The walls behind her were fading away so as to reveal a bizarre, otherworldly landscape that was cold and desolate. Lit in deep blues and electric greens, it resembled a mad painter's vision of the burial ground at Hangman's Hill, crowded with decaying tombstones and crumbling ossuaries. Aunt Rebecca threw down her book and picked up a golden scepter, which she raised above us as she began to utter grotesque language. The words that vomited from her had a tremendous power over me. I found myself bending over unwillingly, getting on hands and knees and assuming a position of supplication before her. Regally, like some daemonic queen, my aunt approached me with the scepter still clasped in her hand, spread her shapely legs far apart, and straddled me like a horse. Shouting her obscene inhuman tongue, she rode me out of the circle of chairs, past the crude bookcases, and out of the room through a wide gap in the transmuted wall, which now dissolved. I carried her on my back over the uneven ground of the graveyard, my burning fingers digging into the dirt for purchase, sharp rocks bruising my knees, for what seemed a great distance until we reached a large stone structure: her awaiting mausoleum.

At that point I awakened, breathing frantically, drenched in sweat—horrified but grateful it had only been a dream. I rubbed my eyes and wondered why my fingers seemed so hot. Reflecting on my vision, I wondered: could there be such a hidden room in this house? Was Lorne correct about my aunt having had a fabulous occult library, and was it still here, in some sequestered place beneath this roof? The answer would have to wait for daylight.

I slept fitfully after that dream, not really resting until the early hours of the morning, at which point—about three a.m. according to the clock on the nightstand—I dropped into a deep sleep that brought blessed oblivion. When I finally came to, it was late morning, the warmth of sunlight leaking around the edges of the window shade flushing my face. My mouth was as dry as a mummy's, and I had a dull headache from not having had my usual dose of caffeine by that hour.

My first unthinking impulse was to conduct a thorough search of all the upstairs rooms, specifically the closets of each bedroom, in quest of the small door of my dream, but I quickly realized I didn't really *want* to find the secret room—if one existed—and I certainly didn't want to discover Rebecca's spooky occult library. That was, in fact, the *last* thing I wanted.

Suppose the dream was true, that there was such a room. How could I possibly see it in a dream? How could an unknown physical reality be revealed by something so intangible and meaningless? For all their splendor and beauty, were not dreams merely random nocturnal hallucinations? A case where a hidden fact was shown to be revealed to the mind through the agency of sleep would be—in itself—a great mystery. But if that was what had really happened, it was a mystery I was in no hurry to solve. I hardly felt up to facing ponderous metaphysical matters so early in the day, and resolved to put the search off for several hours, if not until the morrow. Thus, I postponed dealing with the whole issue for the time being, deciding instead to have a long, leisurely breakfast in town.

While this might seem like cowardice or laziness on my part, it was truly difficult for me to reconcile the two opposites that coexisted in my mind. On the one hand was the feral image of the oppressive, controlling, ruthless beast that my aunt had displayed herself to be in the dream, while on the other hand was my cherished memory of her as a bubbly, fun-loving woman who filled my childhood visits with wonder and delight. Could the truth of the situation be that much different from its surface appearances? I shuddered at the possibility that beneath the mundane world we inhabit in our everyday life there exists a realm haunted by malevolent spiritual lurkers who would destroy us mere mortals in a heartbeat, without hesitation. Something so coldly monstrous that it answers not even to God. In the face of such a thing, my memories of what seemed from all indications to be a normal familial relationship between a great-aunt and her nephew might be meaningless.

I picked a place I'd heard about and had been meaning to try, the Hobo Bean Coffee Company, a hangout for college kids on the corner of Church and Peabody, a couple of blocks from the university. The atmosphere was exactly what I needed at the moment: pleasantly noisy with conversation and the clinking of silverware and dishes, its airy wood-lined spaces filled with golden sunlight and the tempting aromas of good food and freshly perked coffee. I placed my order at the front counter and then took a table in the back of the dining area to wait while my meal was being prepared.

Seeing the waitresses and busboys rushing about, hearing the constant clatter of forks and spoons against ceramic plates and cups, and then a sudden glimpse into the steamy kitchen for just a second when a door swung open and just as quickly shut itself, filled me with a pang of nostalgia for the old days when I'd worked in a restaurant. As much as I enjoyed my inherited wealth and newfound leisure, there was something about having a job that I missed. A feeling that I belonged to the great race of women and men, the common herd who struggled each day for their small share of life's bounty. There were times I truly longed to return to work, but I knew that it would be false because I no longer had the need or the drive it takes to hang in there and continue the grind, day after day. I put it out of my mind as a foolish fantasy; working as a dishwasher or prep cook again when I had a fortune in the bank was a ridiculous idea.

Over by the kitchen, I spotted a bench with complimentary newspapers stacked on it, the type you read and then leave behind for other patrons. I went over and grabbed a copy of Arkham's only surviving newspaper, *The Advertiser*, one that was still nicely folded and hadn't been savaged by previous customers. Inside there was a "Look Back"-style feature article about the devastating storm and flood of 1980. The flood had destroyed much of the docks area, and all of the ancient warehouses down on the waterfront had to be replaced, but—according to the article— the damage wasn't nearly as extensive as was popularly believed. Most of the water-damaged structures in the downtown business district had been salvageable, with only a few being beyond repair and subsequently demolished, in every case being replaced with modern buildings. Of course, virtually all of the homes on French Hill had escaped serious harm and suffered only minor wind damage. My aunt's house had only slight damage to the roof, and one window had been broken by flying debris. Perhaps the worst hit, aside from the waterfront, was Miskatonic University. Thanks to some federal disaster relief money, the University was able to conduct a massive rebuilding program during the '80s, and now the campus was as fully functional as it had ever been.

The same woman who had taken my order called out "Richard!" and I went and got my plate of food and cup of coffee at the pick-up counter. When I returned to my table, the newspaper was already gone, someone apparently having assumed I was finished with it. I sat and turned my attention to eating breakfast. When I'd finished one of my two eggs and was starting on the buttered toast, someone I recognized from my attendance at the poetry readings appeared from out of the crowd and approached my table. Her name was Penelope Armitage. Her claim to fame was that she was the granddaughter of Henry Armitage, a renowned librarian at the University, and she had followed in his footsteps, working her entire adult life as a cataloguer in the same institution. I knew her better as a minor local poet and the long-time Master of Ceremonies at the Desolate Café poetry events. Penelope was what they used to call a spinster. She was unmarried, would remain so, and probably had never even been on a date with a man, let alone slept with one. Short and morbidly thin, she couldn't have weighed over eighty pounds. Her face, which according to old photos I'd seen in poetry journals had once been pleasant enough, if plain, was now ravaged with wrinkles, and her shoulder-length mousy brown hair was streaked with gray. The most memorable and annoying thing about Penelope was her shrill, scratchy voice. Whenever she spoke I had an irresistible urge to clear my own throat, as if doing it for her.

"Well, good sir," she rasped, "fancy meeting you here! I'm more used to seeing your kind face in the crowd at the Desolate than in this establishment."

"Hello, Penelope. Good to see you. Actually, this is my first time here. Thought I'd check it out."

"Well, I suppose the food is acceptable, just barely, and the coffee won't kill you, but I must say that unfortunately the service is on the slow side."

I gestured for her to take the chair beside me and she did so, smoothing her long wool skirt over bony thighs with outspread fingers as she settled onto the cushion.

"Perhaps it is," I said. "I didn't mind, as I was engrossed in a newspaper story."

"That fluff piece on the flood? The hack reporter failed to say that the contractors doing the repairs at Miskatonic took the public for a ride on that deal. Not only was there shoddy workmanship and inferior materials in the construction, but outright fraud with kickbacks from the contractors to the administrators managing the contracts, not to mention the city inspectors looking the other way on code violations—it was quite a scandal!"

"No, they didn't mention that part."

"Makes my blood boil. I had a friend in the business office at the time and the things she observed … well, she could have put several men in jail if she had turned whistle-blower."

"Was anything ever done about it?"

"Nothing. They got away with murder. You know how government works. You scratch my back, I'll scratch yours. Turn the other cheek. Look the other way. It's a corrupt world we live in. Nothing is as it seems."

I wished she hadn't said that last part, for it brought back to mind the dream about my aunt. I tried to steer the conversation in a different direction. "Did you know my aunt Rebecca very well?" Her brows suddenly arched high, exposing crows'-feet in the weathered flesh around the eyes.

"Oh, no. Not well. Not nearly as well as some of our local poets knew her. Rebecca was always somewhat removed from me and my circle of associates. She was—how to put it—something of a literary celebrity, in addition to being a film star. She had studied under the 'great' Edward Derby—I use the term facetiously. She had been his close friend, and his wife's confidante. Rebecca was a privileged insider among the Miskatonic University bohemians, both in Edward's day and later, when she alone ruled supreme among their ranks. I had no access to that crowd. Not with my formal academic background and sense of decorum. Rebecca and her friends did not see me as someone who would fit in among their group. I was establishment, legitimate. I didn't meet their standards of bohemianism. I was not debauched, if you'll pardon my being blunt."

"Really? You were not accepted by the bohemians because of your education and … ah … standards? But, from what I've heard, Derby and his wife, Aesnath, met at the university and were involved with the literati there, the artistic types, the esthetes. Wouldn't that make them, and Rebecca, later, all the more sympathetic and welcoming to a trained scholar like yourself?"

She sniffed. "Not at all. Edward and his bunch, including— I'm sorry to say—your aunt when she was young, were *at* the University but not *of* the University. The Derbys were there to 'party.' That's what I've heard from those who observed them

29

firsthand. They were not serious students. I don't think they were even enrolled in classes!"

"Really? That's surprising."

Her tone became condescending. "Not so surprising. There are the workers, the doers in this world—and then there are those who feed off of the workers, who are always looking for a handout, a free lunch. I put Edward and his wife in that second category. I'm afraid they were a negative influence on Rebecca, as they were on so many of Arkham's youth."

"Indeed. So you said some of the poets who come to the Desolate events did know Rebecca well. Anyone I'd be familiar with?"

"You spoke to one of them at the last meeting. Followed her out, if I recall, although I won't ask what that was all about."

"You mean Julia Spencer?"

"The same. And that Lorne fellow who was bothering you about buying some books, copies of Rebecca's poetry collection. He knew her fairly well. They both did, at one time. They were considerably younger then. I'd say it was around 1970? Something like that."

"Really?"

"I kid you not. My impression is that Ms. Spencer and Mr. Lorne both aspired to be accepted into the inner sanctum of Rebecca's 'circle,' shall we call it, but neither was successful and both were rebuffed. Rebecca was an exclusive one. She didn't open up to just any Johnny-come-lately. She had her private side. With her, there was a line most people could not cross. And try as they might, Julia and Wilus just could not get very far with Rebecca. She used them for a while and then threw them away like Kleenex."

With that, Penelope excused herself, saying she had a meeting of the Arkham Poetry Society to attend. She was the group's secretary, a position she'd held for many years. I bid her farewell and then went and pumped myself a free refill from one of the House Blend decanters and took it out with me to sit at one of the outside tables where I could pass the time watching strangers—mostly college students in their early twenties—walking by on the unimaginable errands of the young.

It was pleasant while it lasted.

My private meditations were interrupted by the sudden appearance of Wilus Lorne, who burst out of the coffee shop carrying in one hand what looked to be a tall mocha to go with two inches of whipped cream on top and what must have been a high-calorie pastry, judging from the grease stains darkening the paper bag holding it. His other hand held tight to his black cane. By the manner in which he held the coffee and bag extended far out in front of him as if to point the way, and speaking with his head twisted back to face me, I knew this was merely passing chatter and not doomed to be a long conversation.

"Pray, what was Prunelope bending your ear about?"

"Oh, nothing. She was trying to tell me that Edward Derby was not a serious student and was only at Miskatonic to party."

Lorne stopped in his tracks and his jaw literally fell in disbelief. "What? She is so full of crap! Derby took a couple degrees while he was there, in what fields, I forget, although she's right about the partying. He didn't let his studies get in the way of enjoying himself. Now his wife Asenath, it's true, wasn't very committed to her studies, especially after she met Edward. And she was quite the party animal herself. Out of control, some say."

"Why would Penelope say something like that?"

"Because she's a frustrated, bitter old hag, seething with jealousy of anyone who is more successful—or happy—than she is. And because she believes all the rumors her old biddy friends tell her."

"Yeah, I had my doubts about what she told me."

"She's full of shit. Don't listen to her," Lorne called out as he limped on.

I spent an hour that afternoon weeding the garden behind the house, quitting when my joints began to ache from being on my hands and knees in the dirt. After washing up and changing into clean clothes, I had a late lunch consisting of a salad with a light balsamic vinaigrette dressing and garlic-flavored croutons and then, in a sudden reversal of mood, decided to look for the secret room. I began in the small room that I had stayed in during my childhood visits, but its closet held nothing more than a box of old toys, some of which I remembered having played with back then. Sorting through them casually, I found one, and then half a dozen grubby, rubber-headed and cloth-bodied hand puppets that filled me with gruesome nostalgia. These grotesque characters— drawn from some long-forgotten children's television program of the 1950s—had been my only playmates when Aunt Rebecca had been too busy with adult business to entertain me and I was left alone in the house to amuse myself. Seeing them again, their leering, too-wide smiles and manic, bulging eyes disturbed me. I shoved them back into the box, face-down, pushing them deep into the layers of stuffed animals and wooden vehicles, and continued my search.

While each of the more elegant, grander bedrooms upstairs had deep walk-in closets like that in my dream, they were all practically bare, having been emptied out when my aunt's clothing was donated to a women's rescue mission after her death. None of the bedroom closets I had gone through at that point had any sign of a door at the back, hidden or otherwise, and I was starting to think the whole idea of a secret room was ludicrous, until I came to the last of the bedrooms upstairs, down a long hallway and around the corner down another, shorter hall. This room's closet had been used by Rebecca to store her possessions other than clothes, including a lot of memorabilia from her films, and was quite full, never having been cleaned out or even inspected after her passing. The closet was so stuffed that I couldn't see the back wall—let alone examine it for secret doors—until I'd carried out twenty cartons of her junk and dragged out three old steamer trunks. Pulling the last of these away freed up a large framed oil painting that had been wedged behind it. The painting was a ghastly scene by an artist whose signature, 'Richard Upton Pickman,' was still legible despite a layer of dust. I set this artistic abomination aside and, turning again to face the wall, discovered there, to my utter shock, a low, small door—exactly like the door in my dream.

The door was not locked. It had been shut for years, and the hinges creaked mournfully as I pried it open, stooped down low enough for my head to clear, and stepped into what proved to be a stuffy, dark, hot enclosure. I could see nothing until I went back down to the kitchen and fetched my little LED flashlight. Once I clicked it on, the intense beam of white light revealed something distressingly similar to the hidden room of the dream: a rough, unfinished space that existed at the intersection of two adjacent bedrooms accessed from different sections of the hallway. The inside walls were the plain backside of lath and plaster, with hardened gobs of rough "brown coat" plaster oozing out in the spaces between the laths. A framework of irregularly sized two-by-fours had been nailed up in a crazy zigzag fashion across these naked lath and plaster walls. The unpainted boards formed a crude bookcase of sorts, one that held what I guessed to be a couple hundred books. There was far too much dust on the books to read any of the spines, but they looked quite old, dating back a century or two, maybe older. The majority had dark leather spines, most of which were crumbling away to expose the bare sewn signatures of the texts. Many of the bindings seemed to have been gnawed by rodents, and the smell of rat excrement was overpowering. That, plus the long-pent-up dust in the windowless space and the stifling heat therein, made the air impossible to breathe, and I found I had to leave after a few minutes of poking around.

I didn't remove any of the books at that time for examination. I had a bad feeling about what their nature might consist of. I resolved that in the days ahead I would take out an armful at a time, blow the dust off them out on the porch, and see what they were about. As if there was any doubt.

I should have known the dirty environment in that closed-up space would play hell with my allergies, and sure enough, half an hour later I was coughing and sneezing, and shortly afterward my sinuses were completely plugged, and I felt totally worthless for the rest of the day. I took an antihistamine tablet and went and lay down in the small bedroom where Rebecca had lulled me to sleep long ago with her dreamy nocturnal tales and sips of the magical liquid in the slim green bottle. The window was still open from the evening before, a gentle wind billowing the curtains. I heard birds singing in the distant trees outside, their cheery trills almost mocking my dark mood. The cool breeze felt refreshing on my feverish face as I lay prone on the small bed, my eyes shut, trying not to think about the reality of what the secret room might mean, and waiting for my sinuses to clear.

Before I knew it, I was asleep and dreaming. The setting was similar to that toward the end of the last dream. We were in the graveyard on Hangman's Hill. Rebecca was in the same shimmering silver gown she'd worn before, the one that was split up the middle so high as to almost expose her intimate parts. I didn't want to feel this, but seeing her shapely thighs and the dark, mysterious recess where the two sides of the gown joined, stirred me in an appalling manner. She had gotten off my back after riding me thus far, and left me there like a despised servant waiting behind for her next command, still on all fours, watching attentively as she lifted the golden scepter to the lightning-cracked sky, uttered an unintelligible alien oath, and strode away.

I continued to watch as the regal Rebecca gracefully ascended a tall stone stairway that led up to a high stone tower. The stairway had been hewn from solid rock ages ago, with wide flat areas of stone forming steps. I was shocked to notice that each of the steps had what looked like a large human-like slug-creature clinging to its top surface, glued into place by a thick coating of secreted mucus. Like the savage queen she was, Rebecca climbed these stairs on the backs of the human slugs, her sharp heels digging deep into the gray translucent flesh of the creatures and inflicting obvious pain upon their sensitive, naked bodies. These bizarre, servile, mollusk-like beings were her acolytes, the aspiring poets who strove to become her favored ones, and I recognized among them none other than my new friends, Wilus Lorne, Julia Spencer, and—most unexpectedly—Penelope Armitage.

These bizarre, servile, mollusk-like beings were her acolytes, the aspiring poets ...

CHAPTER FOUR

O ver the next three days I sought to air out the hidden room by opening all of the bedroom doors and windows upstairs and placing electric fans at strategic locations. Once the atmosphere had freshened up considerably, I gave the space a thorough vacuuming, having illuminated the area by means of an extension cord powering one of the nightstand lamps from the adjoining bedroom. In my aunt's time, the unwired space had been lit solely by candles, as evidenced by the puddles of hardened wax on the floor in several locations. The removal of decades' worth of dust and rodent debris from the floor revealed that—as seen in my precognitive dream—a number of chairs had formerly been positioned around the periphery of the room; their legs had worn circular scars into the painted wood surface of the floor, four telling marks where each chair had stood.

The books I extracted over the course of the next few days were indeed occult in nature. The first batch out seemed relatively tame, being mostly works by the notorious practitioner of black magick, Aleister Crowley, and others about the Order of the Golden Dawn, all published in the early twentieth century. The batch after that consisted of nondescript-looking works in Latin, German and French—none of which languages I could read. I set these aside, thinking I would translate their titles later. They all contained the kind of esoteric symbols and diagrams that you find in run-of-the-mill metaphysical works. So far, none of these books were too disturbing, and none of them caused me to fear that the demonic impression of Aunt Rebecca that I had gained from my dreams had any foundation in reality. Many intellectually curious people have books like these; it doesn't mean they are pursuing evil ends. However, all of my confidence in the benevolence and normalcy of my aunt was shattered by the third and fourth armfuls I carried out of that damnable room. These were much older, mostly leather-bound tomes, some of them fitted with brass corners and clasps on the boards, and they were of a far more sinister nature. Among them were a frightful translation of the *Book of Eibon*, von Junzt's troubling *Unausspechlichen Kulten*, translated into English under the title *Nameless Cults*, the eerie *Dhol Chants*, Balfour's blasphemous *Cultes des Goules* in a rare original French edition, and a fragmentary manuscript of John Dee's English translation of Abdul Alhazred's abhorrent *Necronomicon*. One item, much more recent and probably dating from the 1940s, was a thick mimeographed collection of prayers to some obscene deity named Kamog, and it held extensive marginalia in Rebecca's handwriting. So it was all true: the unsettling dreams I'd had since moving into her house, the whispered rumors about her unsavory connections and wild doings that I'd heard at the poetry readings, Wilus Lorne's insistent claims about an extensive occult library having been in her possession and what that implied. There was no getting around it. My great-aunt had practiced the dark arts, and here was her library to prove it.

Rather than reshelve these books in the hidden room, I decided I would store them in a large walk-in pantry built off of the kitchen. I figured if Lorne ever got snooping around the house, he would surely search the upstairs bedrooms and closets, as well as the library and study downstairs, but I doubted he would even think about looking in the pantry, which conveniently had a locking door. The books would be safe there. I would show them to no one, tell no one about them, and would continue to deny their existence and the existence of the hidden room to Lorne. These regrettable facts would be my burden alone.

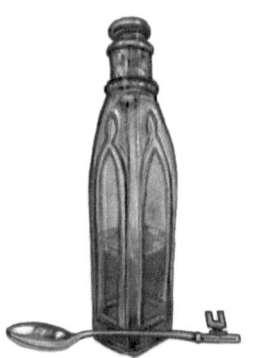

CHAPTER FIVE

I stood on the rooftop terrace of my aunt's house and watched the sunset over the roofs and lanes and river of Arkham. I cannot remember having witnessed a more vibrant sunset, with its intense shades of reds and golds and purples and curious greens. It was, indeed, transporting, and I was reminded again of what a singular town this was—this town of age-old secrets and hidden ways. Perhaps it affected me this way because I was a stranger, an outsider; but I sensed that there was something here that evaded common logic or sensible reality, something that was rare and subtly dangerous. How the queer aura of the town could affect the sky above it I could not comprehend, and yet there was something vaguely outré in the violet mist that coiled far above me. Peculiar fragrances wafted to me, and I could feel the shifting light of day playing on my eyes. I was disturbed—and entranced. I scanned the city and then remembered that there would be another poetry reading at the Desolate Café. Entering the house, I grabbed a light jacket and drove to the north side of town.

Twilight descended as I journeyed to my destination, and after parking my car, I paused before strolling to the café. Witch-haunted Arkham had cast its peculiar spell on me, and my senses were heightened. I could hear the wind sighing through trees, the sound of which had never been more coaxing, as if I were being called to some strange providence. I had parked a few blocks from the Desolate, so as to walk past the ancient houses, some stately and others crumbling from neglect. New England was so singular compared to the boring environment where I had spent the majority of my years. The air tasted of something from the potent past, a vestige of which still lived as an invisible sign that coaxed playfully and poignantly. There were odors on the gentle wind that smelled like nothing I had heretofore drunk in, a combination of fragrances that were a surfeit of sweetness and rottenness. What struck me was that everything I was experiencing had a dream-like quality, as if these senses were not located in bald reality. It was like being attuned to something *other*.

I approached the Desolate Café and entered, and my weird mood did not dissipate. The dull lighting of the place felt weird as it touched my eyes; my enhanced sense of smell was assaulted by human stench—and by something less than human. The homeless poet, Julia Spencer, was sitting at a table in a dusky corner and seemed to be writing on the back of her hand with a silver pen; it was only when I moved nearer that I realized she was etching into her flesh with a small silver dagger. A half-drained cocktail glass rested on the table just beside her hand. She looked up at me and growled "Nar" in a low throaty voice.

I moved away to the bar and ordered a glass of pinot noir, and then I heard my name called out. Wilus Lorne sat at one of the larger tables with a horde of occultists dressed in black. Lorne, ever the dandy, was dressed in a red suit and bowler hat, and his smiling lips wore a hint of crimson gloss. He raised his manicured hand and summoned me again, and so I nonchalantly strolled to their table and returned Lorne's smile.

"We've just been reminiscing about your aunt, Pascal. Some few of us were privileged to have witnessed her rare readings here. Your hand is empty of any volume, dear boy, and we had so hoped that you'd be doing a wee reading yourself, from Rebecca's oeuvre."

How boring they suddenly seemed, these sable-attired poseurs. How little they had to do with any authentic Arkham vibration. I envisioned them in some cellar or on some shadowed hill, chanting in a circle as they slit the throat of an innocent feline, thinking themselves so diabolic. "What are you drinking, Lorne?"

He held up his glass. "A rather tame absinthe cocktail. Care for a sip?" He seemed surprised when I bent to him and took a sip from the proffered glass, when I stayed close to him and blew upon his eyes.

"Do you see visions, dear fellow?" I asked, with a slightly mocking imitation of his vocal tone.

"I'm seeing one now," he muttered, frowning at me suspiciously. He then quickly changed the subject. "We saw you trying to extend your friendly hand to Miss Spencer. I've been buying her drinks all night, she was looking so sad and lost. Ah, but speak of Hecate—there she goes, preparing to read. This may prove amusing." He and his little group burst into laughter as Julia stumbled drunkenly and almost fell.

Sickened by the little clique, I walked to the homeless poet and offered her my hand, and I was pleasantly surprised by the genuine smile with which she graced me as she nodded her thanks and linked her arm with mine. We moved past the rows of chairs where many patrons had congregated and I released my hold on her and turned toward the crowd. "Ladies and gentlemen, may I present a poet of authentic voice and vision, the talented Miss Julia Spencer." Some few applauded my introduction, and I moved and fell into a vacant chair. Julia took a paper from a pocket of her ratty coat and unfolded it, and then she began to sway a little, which filled me with apprehension. Muffled snickering came from someplace in the room, and Julia raised her bleary eyes to peer beyond the rows of chairs. Oddly, she smiled, as the lighting in the room began to dim. The room grew silent as an earthy aroma wafted from the bent and nodding woman before us. Julia ceased her swaying and stood erect, and a soft light came into her eyes that reminded me of something—and then I remembered the unusual light that hovered over some of the tombstones in the Old Wooded Graveyard. Some chilly thing kissed my flesh.

The poet stood in a way that made her look taller than she normally appeared, and the muted, moving shadows of the room worked to alter her facial features. She silently studied the people in the room, and sometimes she smiled queerly at some individual and quietly spoke their name. Seeming to become aware of the paper in her hand, she raised it to her eyes and studied its lines of verse, and then, dropping the sheet to the floor, she parted her lips and began to speak.

> "Step beyond the other side and laugh,
> Step between the space of light and dark.
> Lift thy silver slipper from its raphe,
> Its ridge that forms a seam between two parts.
> Between two parts of being I awake.
> Awakened, I take in the midnight air.
> I move between two realms so to partake
> Of lunacy discovered here and there.
> Here and there I sing to midnight storm,
> Sing to all the elements of earth.
> I smoothly glide, a pale and weightless form,
> A shadow freak, exultant with new birth.
> With novel birth I breathe your mortal name,
> And with chill lips your kisses I reclaim."

The poet shut her eyes and raised both arms, as if to gather souls. Tilting back her head, she pursed her lips and began to whistle an uncanny tune. I was aware of the figure who approached the place where the poet stood, and saw Wilus Lorne stop just before her. Not moving, not opening her eyelids, Julia said, "Come, Wilus—let me kiss thine eyes." Lorne, sans cane, moved closer to her and she wrapped him in her arms, lowering her shadowed face. Her mouth pressed against Lorne's visage for many moments, and when at last she released him, he fell to the floor in a faint. I joined a few others in rushing to him, and someone took out a handkerchief to press against the place on the back of Lorne's head that was bleeding. I took in the smell of blood, and the odor of age-old earth. The poet regarded me peculiarly as she stepped close and smoothed one hand through my hair. "How you've grown," she sighed. I could not move as she swept past me, into the delirium of shadows that seemed to whirl all around.

I could not comprehend this sudden transition in Julia— from a pathetic, low-class character who would be comic were she not tragic in her degradation and debasement, to a figure of mystery, charisma, and power. In her wake, she left behind a potent fragrance that lingered in the café air, one that was unexpectedly sweet and enticing, like the delicate perfume of rose petals, bearing none of the rank vulgarity of her customary aroma of just moments before. She even looked taller, more willowy and sweeping in her movements. It was as if her very soul had somehow been radically altered, her essential nature changed, a finer being substituted for the lesser one that normally inhabited her body.

Lorne, having recovered from his swoon and fall, took advantage of the short intermission between Julia's recital and the next poet listed on the open mic sign-up sheet to saunter with exaggerated nonchalance over to the bar for a refill on the green concoction he was drinking. He was trying to act as if nothing had happened, but I could tell he was rattled, thrown by the spell Julia had cast over him with a single kiss. He appeared embarrassed by the incident, and I suspected that he was eager to have it forgotten.

"Well, Lorne," I teased, "looks like Julia has a fan in you."

"Bah!" he snorted. He took a quick sip of his absinthe, choked on it silently, and then turned away as if determined to rejoin his occultist crew. Halfway to their table he stopped abruptly, as if reconsidering his destination, and took a detour over to my table instead, where he remained standing. "Any luck in finding Rebecca's stash of grimoires, Richard?"

"What? Oh, no—I haven't looked. I really doubt she had such a collection of occult books. It's not consistent with her personality and interests as I knew them. But if she did, I suspect they were disposed of long ago, well before her death."

"I beg to differ, my dear fellow; she did indeed have just such a collection of books, I assure you of that. I have it on good authority." With that last, he rolled his eyes melodramatically and then looked away with arched brows, as if to suggest that merely knowing the source of this privileged information would both startle and terrify me.

I played his game. "And who might that be?"

"Never you mind, dear boy. Also, you must know, she was rumored to have had a secret room in the house where meetings of her select group of acolytes—her so-called 'chosen ones'—were held. Candles burned, rituals performed, prayers to dark deities offered up, that sort of thing. You've found this room, haven't you." From his tone, this was a statement of fact and not a question.

I laughed mildly. "There's no secret room, Wilus. Your imagination has gotten the better of you. Don't you think if there was a 'secret' room in her house, I'd have found it by now?"

"Exactly. I believe you have."

"You'd better return to your seat. The next reader is about to begin."

This second poet was introduced by Penelope Armitage, who had arrived late, in a fluster, and missed Julia's performance altogether. His name, as Penelope announced in her scratchiest tone, was Peter Franklyn, and he was the son of Ronald Franklyn, a well-known British cult leader of the 1960s and author of an obscure volume titled *We Pass from View*. Peter was a lanky fellow of about fifty, sporting a long beard and longer hair, the latter neatly tied in a ponytail that hung down the back of his corduroy sports coat. Taking the stage, he pulled a handful of crumpled manuscript pages from his suede leather backpack, sorted through them at length, and finally selected a poem from which he read in a strong melodious voice.

> "They say that Arkham was overrun
> by witches in days gone by,
> but nightly on her cobbled streets
> I still see crones pass by,
> and younger, more comely practitioners
> of ye dark arts I may spy,
> lingering in shadowed doorsteps
> under an eerie and mottled sky."

The poem went on from there, but I stopped listening the second I noticed Julia leaving with Lorne's band of black-attired occultists in tow, the lot of them shuffling noisily through the dark café toward the back door. By the time I exited the place, Julia and her crowd were halfway down the next block. Of course, I really didn't know where they were headed but quickly surmised it must be Hangman's Hill. Just as Julia had gone there after her reading the last time, she was likely headed there again. The graveyard there, it seemed, was her only home.

It was fully dark now, the mystical ambivalence of what had been a glorious Arkham twilight sadly departed from the scene.

The street lamps—spaced widely apart—provided just enough illumination for me to detect the forms of Julia, Lorne and his associates advancing ahead of me one street down, but I could not make out their individual features. It was clear which one was Julia—she was at the lead and was the shortest of the lot, plus her long skirt marked her as the group's only female; and it was equally obvious which of them was Lorne, thanks to his outfit's red hue (which, in the dim light, appeared as a ruddy brown, compared to the jet black of the occultists' attire) and his walking-stick. They were somewhat more than silhouettes, but barely so, with only the vaguest of details of their forms being distinguishable to my aged eyes. Overhead, brilliant stars pierced the blind spaces between the gloomy trees, lending the night sky an icy poignancy. The group was moving quickly, and I found I needed to walk at a brisk pace to keep up. Although I knew no good reason why I should conceal myself from them, I did so, staying far enough behind that I doubted they would take any notice of being followed. Julia had them all transfixed. That much was clear by the way they swarmed about her whenever she slowed for a second and turned to utter something to one of them—phrases whose meaning I could not make out, although the indistinct music of her voice did reach me, carried on the cool breeze.

Although I had followed the poet once before, at that time I was under some kind of spell, oblivious to time and place. This time I was wide awake and fully in self-control. After what seemed like a long walk across a significant portion of Arkham, we began to go uphill, first gradually so, and then rather abruptly, until we were involved in a steep climb, and I began to get winded and broke into a sweat. Thankfully, they were too far away to hear my huffing and puffing. I yearned to stop and catch my breath, but didn't dare, fearing I would lose sight of them; so I pressed forward, the strain of which effort I felt more than was comfortable. Finally, we reached a plateau—from the view of the city over my shoulder I knew this must be Hangman's Hill—and the path leveled off. As before, when on the night of the first poetry reading I'd followed Julia out here, we came to a derelict old iron fence. I saw them scrambling over a low and bent section of it and decided that was the best spot for me to scale it as well, but only when they were well ahead of me again, for I'd caught up a bit with them while they were climbing the fence two at a time, and had closed the gap between us considerably.

From the fence, they headed off into a field that was so overgrown with tall, dry grass that their legs were hidden and I only saw their bodies from the waist up, and as we got deeper into the grass, only their heads and shoulders were visible. In my exhausted state, it took me longer than it should have to get over the fence, and I cursed under my breath at my slowness, lest I lose sight of them altogether. At first, the field was uninterrupted yellow grass, but as I penetrated farther into the burial grounds, I encountered a motley assortment of weathered and broken headstones and neglected larger granite and marble monuments. Eventually, the grass thinned out and the grave markers increased until I was in the graveyard proper. Without the grass to provide cover, I had to stay back a considerable distance from Julia and her group to avoid detection. Dodging from side to side, I found I was able to keep some of the taller monuments between us, which provided me some cover.

Thus, I followed them far into the cemetery until we reached the section where Rebecca's stately tomb was situated, and to see it in reality sent a wave of chilliness through my being. She had built this impressive mausoleum while still a relatively young woman, using a sizable portion of the wealth she had accumulated as a motion picture star. At the time, Arkham's newspaper columnists had found the story irresistible, luridly asking why a woman who was apparently in good health and had every reason to expect a long life ahead of her would spend the lion's share of her fortune on something as morbid as a family sepulcher. One gossip who knew Rebecca better than the others hinted that my aunt had developed her macabre fixation on mortality shortly after befriending Edward and Asenath Derby, and furthermore suggested that the Derbys had somehow exerted an "unnatural influence" over Rebecca.

At any rate, Rebecca had seduced the city officials into letting her purchase this section of the otherwise disused graveyard, and she had spared no expense in constructing the tomb, which was built of solid Italian marble and occupied a central position in one of the more exclusive sections of the burying ground. I had found many photos of the structure when exploring my great-aunt's house—in many of which she had posed in front of it over the years, in stately film-goddess stance—and I had always been made uncomfortable by the fact that the heavy stone door—which hung on ornate iron hinges—was chained shut, as if either to keep out intruders (a more likely scenario), or, to hold captive the souls therein interred. While I had not been present for Rebecca's funeral, I had heard from family members that my aunt had arranged to have the remains of her deceased parents disinterred and relocated to a crypt in the mausoleum only a few months before her own death, and then, when she unexpectedly passed, was herself laid to rest beside them in the same vault.

Julia and her band of followers came to a stop at the tomb, and the occultists formed a circle around the poet as she turned to face them and me. I abruptly halted and hid behind a mossy sculpture of a sad angel that marked the final resting place of one of Arkham's leading citizens from the 1880s. Peeking carefully around the edges of this melancholy memorial, I was able to watch the scene without much chance of their seeing me in return. I was close enough to hear parts of Julia's oratory as she addressed the assembly in a melodramatic tone that, oddly, reminded me of the speeches my aunt Rebecca used to give in her films when the heroine she played had come to a critical point in the story.

"And *this*," Julia cried. throwing out her left arm and pointing with a long, elegant index finger to Rebecca's grand sepulcher, "this is *my* tomb, where I lie in dreamy slumber awaiting the glorious time when I shall rise up again from the merciless clay and ascend to the stars with my Awful Master!"

Hearty cheers and ecstatic sighs rose from the occultists, while Lorne, letting loose of his walking stick, fell humbly to his knees and bowed his head in supplication to Julia, his arms outstretched before him and his palms pressed firmly to the cold, pebbled soil.

"You, my loyal subjects, *you* will join me there! At the appointed moment, I shall gather you up and exalt you! You shall share in my glory and forever enjoy the protection and pleasure of my Lord, His Beastliness—you know the one I mean, don't you, my eager ones?"

And with that they all cried rapturously as with one voice, repeating over and over a bizarre name I had heard or read somewhere recently but which I could not at the moment place: "Kamog! Kamog!" they cried, "On high! In the clouds! Great and wondrous, O Kamog!"

Julia eyed Lorne as he genuflected before her, and then she bent to him and placed both of her hands on his left leg. He shuddered in ecstasy and began to weep, and everyone else cried out euphorically. This wild exchange between Julia and the occultists went on for a good while, and then the light shifted as if a cloud had passed before the disk of the moon, and the air grew colder. The call-and-response ceased with the occultists' voices trailing off in weakened enthusiasm. As the hubbub died down, a change came over Julia. She seemed to cave in on herself, to shrink in size and stateliness, as if all the air had been sucked from her lungs. She then collapsed in a heap beside Lorne and resumed her everyday appearance as a nondescript lost soul, a pathetic little homeless woman in rags, all of the charm and charisma she had assumed at the poetry reading having vanished. Any power she held over the group was suddenly gone as well, and they felt this at once, turning away from her in disinterest and wandering off into the tall grass under the occluded moonlight. Julia herself drifted away, cackling idiotically and fishing in her pockets for a cigarette which she lit with a disposable lighter. Soon, only Wilus remained in my view, still down on his knees. He presently got up, dusted himself off, turned in my direction and saw me—without much interest, it seemed—as I had come out from behind the statue of the sad angel and was now in plain sight. He approached, head cast down, looking disoriented from what he had just experienced, and as he walked I noticed that he had lost his limp.

Raising his eyes to mine, he spoke firmly in a tone that was unmistakably hostile. "You saw it, Richard. Don't deny it! You saw her manifest here before us tonight! She is mighty, and her powers increase. There's nothing you can do to stop her, nor us. We will have our way, with or without your cooperation. Julia Spencer's days are numbered."

Then he turned and walked off into the dead grass that swayed gently in the cool nocturnal breeze. I felt frightened and alone, quite uneasy about staying any longer in that terrible place. I moved and groaned at the stiffness in my joints, the weakness of my limbs. Looking where Lorne had dropped his walking stick, I staggered to the spot and picked up the cane. It would assist me on my long walk home.

CHAPTER SIX

⌐—▼—⌐

The bizarre scene on Hangman's Hill was so unsettling that I could not sleep when I first arrived home later that night. I decided I would select a volume from among those of Rebecca's books I'd hidden in the pantry and take it upstairs to bed with me so I might read myself to sleep. The book I chose for this purpose was one that did not look in any way sinister or archaic, as did the others, and thus I reasoned it would not draw undue attention from anyone who might come snooping about the house looking for Rebecca's occult library. It was a rather primitive mimeographed volume of cult lore that appeared to be from the 1940s or 1950s. The book was printed in purple ink on multi-colored sheets, which were contained in a screw-post binder with fake leatherette covers. There was no identification on the spine, and only a small paper label on the front cover providing a title, typed in all-caps: *INCANTATIONS OF KAMOG*. It wasn't until I had propped myself up on a pile of pillows and had the volume spread open in my lap that I recalled the strange words I'd overheard earlier that evening at Rebecca's tomb, the cryptic chanting of the occultists, who repeatedly used that same odd name, "Kamog." So *that's* where I'd seen the name before: here on this very book. According to the title page, the book had been published in Innsmouth by a group identifying itself as "The Loyal Followers of the Late Asenath Waite Derby." No date of publication was given, and no copyright was claimed. This was clearly my great-aunt's personal copy, as it was heavily annotated with extensive marginalia in her hand.

Comfortably positioned as I was, the time flew by as I read through a good fifty pages in an effort to get the gist of the volume. The text was mostly incantatory verses that were meant to be recited during magical rituals. These were interspersed with short prose passages that provided instructions for the use of the verses, along with admonishments, warnings, tips, and background information. As best I could tell, the material was a chaotic mix of original writings by Asenath, her husband Edward Derby, and members of their group, along with older traditional texts cribbed from obscure occult publications and manuscripts, with no printed attributions for any of this material, although the sources were often noted by Rebecca in her distinctive handwriting.

The windows of the bedroom were open, and a cool breeze teasingly billowed the curtains as I softly mouthed the strange verses over and over to get the proper feel of them. I was hoping this reading would give me a better understanding of my aunt's life and mind, maybe even that I would discover some redeeming aspect of the ideas expressed in the book that would cast my aunt in a better light than that in which recent events had shown her. Something like mercy, kindness, universal love, good will, tolerance—any positive human emotion or motive would do the trick—but I found nothing of the sort. It was all darkness, greed, lust, and selfishness. There were no redeeming thoughts to be found in the book. It was a bible of evil, a testament of vanity. Weary of the relentless striving for power inherent in the text and indicative of the emotional poverty of the minds behind it, I threw the volume across the room in disgust—not violently but almost tenderly, lobbing it into a corner where it hit the plaster wall with a dull thud and collapsed into a jumble of rainbow-colored pages, its binding having been broken by the force of the impact. The curtains gently stirred once more, as before, and then without any warning, they suddenly billowed out in fullness as a much stronger wind flooded the room, like some great volume of air rushing in to fill a vacuum.

Outside I heard a sort of woody thrashing noise that brought me to my feet and to the window. I swept aside the unruly curtains and beheld a scene of unbelievable madness in the landscape. Every tree in the neighborhood was in wild motion, swaying frantically back and forth, the limbs of some even whipping up and down as if by the hand of some malevolent giant. The birds—I suppose they were whippoorwills—were in a panic, all calling at once in a shrill cacophony of avian anarchy. Small furry animals—rodents, squirrels, and the like—darted across the lawns in great confusion. It was as if Nature herself had sounded an alarm that something was terribly amiss in the world. An icy cold wind blasted my face and bare arms with its full force, frightening and yet thrilling me at the same time, and flashes of lightning illuminated the dark sky and backlit the silhouettes of the weirdly animated trees. I didn't know whether to tremble in fear or in exaltation. And then, without any sort of transitional state, it was much later, and I was asleep, in total darkness, on the bed, slowly struggling up from oblivion and finding my way back to consciousness from a most blasphemous nightmare.

The dream was fresh in memory. I was one of the supplicants humbly approaching the grotesquely transformed Rebecca. She appeared to be some sort of exotic fertility goddess, such as you would find in the obscene sculptures carved on an ancient stone temple in India. She was seated on a low, gray, wet, lichen-clotted rock wall, with her heavy thighs splayed wide and her arms held out in a frog-like posture. But what she resembled more than frog or toad was the hybrid of a giant octopus and a woman. This resemblance was the immediate effect of the purplish-white hue of her naked flesh, especially on the inner thighs where the skin was

... in a panic, all calling at once in a shrill cacophony of avian anarchy.

mottled and bubbled with a great many pale, whitish warts. But the most appalling and shocking aspect of her transfigured body was in the pelvic region. Instead of the normal human female organs of generation, she possessed a huge, almost cavernous vagina, the labia thick as an elephant's skin and riddled with deep cracks and fissures, the surface of the skin there soiled and hardened until it bore a dull, burnished sheen. Everything about this central disfiguration suggested gross abuse and excessive, even morbid usage over a prolonged period of time—whether for procreation or libidinous pleasure-seeking it was impossible to say. I was horrified by this sight, but literally could not turn away. It was only after perhaps a half minute of observing this lewd display that I noticed the long, writhing tentacles that extended around from behind her full hips and undulated towards us, her supplicants, as if to draw us inward to her. In one terrible moment, several thinner tentacles curled up backwards from her hips, touched her painted eyelids and then penetrated her skull, sliding past the whites of her rolled-up eyes, and at that point in the dream I passed out, awakening to reality in a frisson of cosmic horror.

This latest grotesque dream about Aunt Rebecca in conjunction with the strange natural phenomena in and around the house earlier that same evening was so disturbing to me that I made a point of doing whatever I could to obliterate it from my mind. In practical terms, this meant busying myself with a thousand mundane tasks and diversions. I balanced my checkbook, cleaned the house, washed the car, weeded the garden, and began reading several books at the same time, all of them light, escapist fare—mystery novels, celebrity biographies, and other equally trashy works. Anything that might take my mind off the ugly horror in that dream. Hanging about the house all day and night wasn't helping any, so I made sure I got out at least once a day to do something—anything—outside of my normal routine. I combined a trip to the post office to mail some bill payments with a visit to a shabby little used-paperback store (the last thing I needed was more books, but I limited myself to browsing without buying.) One afternoon, I went to a trendy gelato shop that I'd read about in the *Advertiser* and enjoyed a delicious, if expensive, double vanilla cone. On the third day after the bad dream, I returned to the Hobo Bean Coffee Company for a late breakfast. It was a weekday and the place was crammed with students—so much so that I could barely find a table once I'd placed my order. I'd just managed to secure a section of the newspaper that looked like it had been rolled up and used to swat flies, when I spied Penelope Armitage headed my way carrying a to-go coffee.

"Ah! Greetings, Penelope."

"Greetings to you, Mr. Pascal. How are you on this fine day?"

"I'm well, thank you. Care to join me?"

She promptly sat down, but remained perched on the edge of her seat with only her toes touching the floor, as if she were about to launch herself into a sprint at any second.

"I'll stay for just a moment," she explained. "I'm on break from work, but there is something I've wanted to talk to you about."

This aroused my interest, perhaps unreasonably so; although there were any number of more mundane things she might wish to discuss with me, for some reason I suspected the topic she had in mind had to do with my great-aunt and her relationship, or lack of one, with the University library.

"What might that be?" I asked, genuinely curious.

"Well, late last week—Friday it was—it was my turn to man the desk in the Rare Book Room. Normally, that's the duty of the reference librarians, but one of them has been out on maternity leave so I and another cataloger have been helping fill in for an hour or two as the need arises. Not terribly challenging work—

taking call slips from patrons, fetching materials for them from the closed stacks and then keeping an eye on them while they use the items at one of the long tables in the Rare Book Room. Mainly you want to be sure they wear white gloves while handling the books and manuscripts and such, and that they only use pencil for note-taking—never an ink pen."

"And …?"

"And a pair of young men came in and asked to see a copy of your Aunt Rebecca's book, *Step into the Moonlight, and Other Poems*. It's a rare first edition, as you know."

"The first and only edition to my knowledge, although a reprint has been discussed."

"Yes, the first and only edition. There was something about the two of them I did not trust. They looked a bit 'sketchy,' if you will, so I kept a close eye on them. At one point, after the youths had perused the volume for about five minutes, pointing fingers at passages and whispering conspiratorially to one another, the seemingly younger of the two—a blond boy who I sensed was a follower type, not a natural-born leader—stood up and placed himself directly between the older boy—who was clearly the one in charge of whatever nefarious mission they were on—and me, thereby cutting off my view of the book which was now in the hands of the older boy. While this in itself could be entirely innocent, it was rendered most suspicious by the fact that at the exact moment in which I could no longer see the book, I heard a distinct ripping sound, as if paper were being torn."

"Seriously? Are you saying they vandalized my aunt's book?"

"Apparently they did. Shortly thereafter, the older of the two returned the book to me, and they left hastily. I immediately checked the volume and found that the leaf bearing pages 58 and 59 was missing—a ragged stub of paper running the length of the gutter between pages 57 and 60 being the only sign it had ever been there."

"Remarkable!" was all the comment I could muster. I couldn't imagine why anyone would want to desecrate my aunt's book.

"While I'm afraid I don't have their names, I do recognize these young rapscallions. A colleague pointed them out to me not long ago and warned me to beware of them, alleging they are high-ranking members of an underground cabal of students notorious for dabbling in the occult. I shared the incident with this same colleague and she believes they may be planning to use the stolen page—or, rather, the verse it bears—in a necromantic ritual they intend to perform to contact the spirit of your deceased aunt. Bit of a wild theory, if you ask me, but this colleague seems to know quite a lot about these shady characters, and who am I to say she's wrong? From certain faculty members, I've heard scandalous rumors about these kids. They have a reputation for throwing wild, all-night parties, excessive drinking, taking hallucinogenic drugs and practicing black magic, not to mention frequent brushes with the law. So, given their deplorable reputation, I thought I should inform you."

This was a lot to take in. "Thank you for confiding in me, Penelope. I really appreciate knowing about this, unsettling as it is. My word, I barely know what to make of it. A very strange business all told. I'll have to give it some serious thought."

"While I suspected the youths of criminal behavior—well, petty larceny—I couldn't prove they removed the page. It very well may have been missing for years when I gave them the book. It's not the sort of thing that would get easily noticed. I only found out about the damage because I was looking for it. Speaking of which, with the library's copy of the book being ruined, by any chance do you have an extra copy you could sell us?"

"I do have a spare copy, but I'll give it to you gratis—a gift to the library."

"Oh, that would be wonderful! Thank you, Richard. You're a scholar and a gentleman."

I smiled, embarrassed by her praise. "It's nothing, really. Let me have the address and I'll mail it to you at the library. You'll have it in a few days."

Again she thanked me, at the same time handing me her business card. Then she rose, patted me almost tenderly on the shoulder, and dashed off, disappearing into a throng of students backlit by the bright sunlight flooding in through the front windows. I flipped her card over and wrote "Page 58/59" on it with the fountain pen I routinely carried in my inside coat pocket. The pen was one I had found on my aunt's desk, a beautiful antique instrument with a nib made of pure 24-carat gold. The ink, a rich brown walnut-colored fluid, was also derived from her desk where a quantity of it resided in a small crystal bottle that looked decades old. I loved writing with this particular ink because it had the exact appearance of the handwriting one often found in antique tomes, writing which had once been a dark blue, or even black, but had faded over the years to a warm, earthy hue.

As much as I appreciated the information, news of the vandalized book only served to remind me of Rebecca and the weird aura of otherness that seemed to cling to her memory. My effort to blot these feelings from consciousness for even a few minutes was a failure.

That evening, I examined pages 58 and 59 in my personal copy of Rebecca's book, curious to learn which poem of hers the rowdy teenagers would be using for their tawdry juvenile ceremony. I was somewhat stunned by the fact that I immediately recognized the poem that fills these two pages, and it was more familiar to me than had it been any other among Rebecca's many poems. Indeed, it was fresh in my mind, for I had read it quite recently. The poem, titled "Arise into the Air Ye Seekers and Join the Living Spirit," also appeared—not credited to Rebecca—in that heinous mimeographed compilation, the *INCANTATIONS OF KAMOG*.

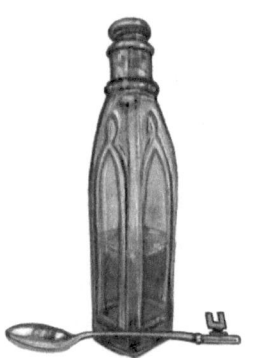

CHAPTER SEVEN

Aunt Rebecca was complacent concerning the collection
of her papers and cinematic props that formed a small
archive at Arkham's university, and never answered the
university's request for additional personal papers, film scripts or
manuscripts of her writing. Having been named in her will as her
literary executor, I felt it my duty to give the choicest of papers
that I found to their collection; and so I inelegantly stuffed a
large cardboard box with the more interesting items and drove
to College Hill and its Miskatonic University. Because the box
was so heavy, I found someone from the library and asked for
the use of a handcart with which to convey the hoard of items
to whomever would arrange their entry into the collection, and I
was rewarded with a muscular young student who accompanied
me to my car and easily carried the box. The curator in charge of
my aunt's collection overflowed with excitement and gratitude,
and I promised that I would search for further items when I had
time.

As my time in Arkham increased, I became more aware
of a curious "flavor" in the air, a cauldron's mixture of history,
magic and scandal. It was like nothing I had ever thought to
encounter, and the longer I lived in my aunt's house, the more
aware I became of her intimate connection to the secrets of
Arkham. A significant element of Arkham's sinister nature existed

at Miskatonic University, and it began to intrigue me to the point where I decided to linger on campus and allow my psyche to soak in the Arkham mystique that I detected there. It was as if there was an undercurrent of cloaked arcane awareness, and I sensed it as I spoke with the library curator. It wasn't obvious in anything that he discussed with me; it was an intangible flavor that one perceived, like some shadow of a presence that existed outside reality as one knew it. Perhaps it was an overreaction of my imagination, but I seemed to notice odd, yet subtle touches in the very design of the ancient buildings that had been erected on the campus grounds, and as I walked, I studied the curiosities of those structures, the queer ways in which some roofs slanted, the suggestive sigils that had been engraved into some few stones with which the buildings had been constructed. I marveled at the duplicity of the thing—how it was concealed in background, and yet when one became attuned to its nature, it was keenly obvious all around.

The sky was slightly overcast, and the sun was a vague circle sheathed in clouds, looking to me like some portal through which one could be transported to another side of sky. I peered at that spectral disc for a long time until my eyesight blurred and my head began to ache. Looking away, I became aware of a black blur advancing toward me on the campus ground, a midnight amoeba spotted with white blobs that, gradually, became faces. Wilus Lorne and a pack of occultists crept toward me. Judging from their very youthful faces, I took these others to be college students, and some of them had been with their shaman at the Desolate Café. A rather ugly young man walked up to me and studied my face.

"Your eyes look haunted, Richard Pascal. You've been studying uncanny things."

Repulsed, I meant to back away from the freak, but he clutched at my arm and held me fast. "I've been staring at the sun, and studying the sigils on some of the buildings, those so-suggestive icons. And who are you, sirrah?"

"Abraham Waite, of Innsmouth." He raised one hand to my face and used a grimy-looking finger to trace a sigil on my forehead. His skin was dry, like the skin of a corpse. Shuddering, I pushed him from me and frowned as the sound of low laughter filtered from the watchers in black attire.

"We saw you with that meaty young fellow who was carrying your box. We are intrigued," Lorne said.

"I've donated some significant papers of my aunt's to the library, for their collection of her works and such. They were of no use to me, and here they will help confirm her reputation as literary artist. Her writing, you know, meant more to her than her success in cinema. Acting was easy for her, almost a form of play; but her writing required thought and effort, and originality."

"There's more to her acting than you might realize," Lorne suggested.

"Ah, how cryptic. Yes, well; I'll leave such esoteric matters to you and your little friends. Good day."

Turning away from the pack of fools, I marched out of the campus to where my car was parked. My mood was not improved when I reached home and found Julia Spencer in the rocking chair on my front porch. I called to her as I climbed the porch steps, but she did not respond to the sound of her name. Reaching out to the chair, I stopped its rocking motion and called her name again. When she turned her face to look at me, I saw that she was in her weird phase of personality; but there was something in her altered eyes that reminded me of someone I used to know. The voice that spoke to me was not that of the homeless poet. I found myself trembling as I whispered, "Aunt Rebecca?"

"Sit beside me, lad, and wipe that foolish expression from your face. I seem to have misplaced my key to the house. Have you yours? Why do you goggle at me like that? It's most unbecoming."

"I don't understand what you are," I said, sitting on the wooden surface beside her chair.

She squinted her eyes as if searching inside her soul, and when she spoke again her voice was very low. "I am the fire of essence that is your aunt, and I have usurped this unhappy vessel by the power of Kamog, an entity that nestles in the pit of my being until, in time, it will blossom and take over, gloriously." She looked down at me and smiled. "You still look astonished. You recognized me, I know."

"Yes."

"Then why do you look so troubled?"

"How the hell am I supposed to look?! Where is Julia?"

She smiled and nodded. "You're becoming fond of the wretch, eh? She nestles in my tomb, in what remains of my fleshy husk. She dreams of worms and ghastly things, and sighs with midnight wind. She's never been happier, or so at peace."

"I want her released."

"You *want.* I have not been long dead, and I am restless. I have plots that need to be accomplished. My creative powers, of which you have gained an inkling, grow forceful, and we have new marvels that beg for conjuring. Your little friend is less than one of the maggots that have frolicked in my hair as I slumber in my stony bed. Forget the wench, and assist me in my art, blood of my blood. There is much that I may teach you. Come, my pet, let me kiss your brow and bestow on you the gift of Arkham witchery, that potent alchemy." I ignored her request, and so she stood and wrinkled her nose. "Does this creature never wash? Pah, the reek. Give me your key, child, and we'll continue this conversation after I've showered."

I didn't want to move, but I could not help but lift my eyes to hers; and the blackness that I saw swimming in her orbs seemed to spill invisibly into me and churn within my soul. I felt haunted and afraid. Digging into my pocket, I produced the key. Taking it, she released me from her spell and entered the house. I don't know how long I sat there before I became aware of a form that lurked near me. Turning my head, I confronted a scowling Wilus Lorne. I could smell booze on his breath as he panted before me.

"You're going to show me the secret room, Pascal. No, don't pretend. You've been visiting this house since childhood, and you've now lived here long enough to learn its furtive wonders. I know that houses are tainted by the powerful souls of the ones who have lived within their walls, and none were more powerful than Rebecca. And you are of her blood." He leaned closer, demanding my attention. "But you were never *devoted* to her as we are. You never *served* her."

I sneered. "Your aggressive tone doesn't intimidate me, Lorne. I don't know what narcotics you've been imbibing—your eyes look shocking. No, you'll remove your drunken carcass from my property. I'll not allow you to defile it with your pretentious Satanism or whatever the hell your game is. Be gone."

He knelt before me on the porch steps, and I hated having his frantic face so near my own. I turned away in an effort to escape the sour stench of his breath and the sight of his red-rimmed eyes. It was shocking to see him in such a state, as he had always presented himself as a carefully immaculate Bohemian dandy. Once a magnificent sunflower, he was now a debauched and drooping lily excreting a noxious bouquet of rottenness. Looking at him again, I felt a stab of pity. Rising, I took his hand and led him inside, to the kitchen, where I brewed a fresh pot of coffee and heated a scone in the microwave. My actions seemed to amaze him, and yet the sight of my offering triggered a response. Buttering his scone, he began to feast. When he picked up the coffee mug with both hands, I saw that he was trembling. "You're very kind," he whispered.

Softly, I laughed. "You speak as if it's strange that I should be so."

Lorne shrugged and drank another mouthful of coffee, and then wiped at his mouth with a napkin that I had provided. "I'm a decadent in Arkham, dear boy. You are an innocent among fiends and freaks. No one can really be as naive as you pretend to be."

I laughed. "Your pose of decadence is a form of adolescent innocence. Wickedness is overrated."

"Show me Rebecca's secret room, Richard. Then I'll expose such authentic wickedness as you could never comprehend. Oh, her sinister power! Her majestic malignity!"

"Why would I desire to be exposed to such a thing? Yes, my aunt was a potent woman—because of her creativity. Her vitality lives on, in her films and her poetry."

Lorne shook his head, signifying that I was a hopeless case. Setting down the mug, he frowned at me for some few moments, and then he turned and left the kitchen. I listened for the sound of the front door to open and close, and when that did not happen I went to investigate. Lorne was standing, silent and unmoving, at the bottom of the stairway. Following his upward gaze, I saw Julia, and gasped at her transformation. Not only had she showered and groomed, but she had found one of the gowns from Aunt Rebecca's film roles and had so adjusted it that it fitted her to near-perfection. A spectacular necklace of what looked like diamonds clasped her throat and reached down to the cleft between her breasts. Although Julia was not a young woman, she looked far more youthful than she had just an hour previously. Like some superb and graceful animal, she descended the stairway and stood before me.

"You've not been very adventurous, Richard. Don't you remember how we used to play with my jewelry when you were but a child? You loved to feel my gems shimmer on your eyes. And yet you've forgotten where I had sequestered my treasure trove." Demurely, she grinned. "Do take your eyes from my cleavage, nephew. Ah, how you blush! This creature had the dust of the ages in her pores. I have thoroughly cleansed her. Why are you here, Wilus?"

"He insists on hunting for your 'secret' room," I replied.

The decadent fellow gaped at me in astonishment. "You know who she is!" Trembling, he knelt before her. Julia winked at me and rolled her eyes.

"Do get up; you look pathetic. Secret room? Ah, my legend carries on. If such a room exists, it's no concern of yours. You were one of my admirers when I lived, and I allowed you to participate in some mild exotic play; but you were never one of my acolytes."

"I am devoted to you, and to the power that is Kamog! I shall worship you as one among your cult of Devoted Ones. Pascal here doesn't understand the power of the Outside. We do!"

The woman's eyes darkened with a kind of cruelty. "We? Do you mean that pack of black-clad poseurs you were with the other night, in the burying ground?" She clucked her tongue cynically and shook her head. "Well, you may be of some use to me, in time. For now—be gone." There was such an element of force in her command that Lorne grew pale with fright, backed away to the door and exited the house. Drawing close, she lifted her hand to my hair and ran fingers through it. "He's correct in one instance: you have no comprehension of the Outside, and its allure. That is something I can teach you. And I will." Bending to me, she kissed my cheek, and I was startled at how familiar that kiss felt. Patting my cheek, she strode out of the house, into darkness.

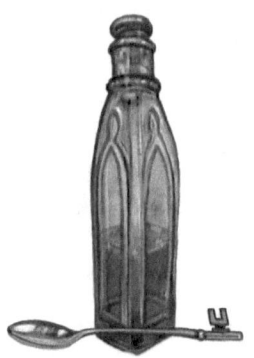

CHAPTER EIGHT

Aunt Rebecca quickly settled into her new existence in
the house, and although I could barely accept the reality
of her miraculous return from the dead, I soon became
used to seeing her as she passed through the rooms that had long
been empty of all but memories and down hallways that—other
than my own infrequent appearances—had remained still and
silent since her interment. She was obsessively occupied with
the seemingly endless preparations for the event she called "my
final ceremony." I seldom imposed upon her with comments
or questions, but let her proceed in peace, lost in a reverie of
anticipation. I refrained from conversation not only because I
felt a great deal of apprehension as to exactly what she really was
now, but also because I wouldn't have known what to say to her
anyway. How does one address a spectre? What does one say to
a spirit that possesses another's body? For as much as I loved my
great-aunt, this entity that swept from room to room speaking
in Rebecca's voice was not a living person. My aunt was dead,
and this was ... something else. What, I did not know. And yet I
sensed her presence there; I felt the power of her mind, and her
love for me. Thoughts such as these troubled my mind for several
days and nights, but I kept them to myself. I suppose I was afraid
to discuss the matter with her, fearing the answers she might give
me.

Early one evening, she stopped abruptly at the top of the stairs and turned to look at me standing below at the base of the stairway, her hands securing the copious folds of her gown so she wouldn't trip on the material.

"Richard, be honest with me. Do you think me too harsh in my treatment of Mr. Lorne? Was I cold in my dismissal of him? I don't want to be an uncaring bitch. My followers should always think of me as a supremely loving mistress. They should revere me as Catholics revere their Virgin Mother, not fear and despise me."

I was startled by the question. She had been cruel to him, it's true. He obviously yearned for nothing more than to serve her and be accepted into her retinue, and yet she hadn't given him the time of day.

"Perhaps," I answered, "you could be a little nicer to him. He's a fool, there's no denying it, but I suspect he means well. He does worship you so, Rebecca."

She sighed. "I've been considering giving him another chance. Even if he proves unworthy of full initiation into our inner sanctum, he might prove useful to us, in some way or other. There's more than one role to be played in this drama. Of course, a key role—a leading part, I'd say—goes to you, my beloved nephew." She smiled at me, and her eyes shimmered. "I have so much to teach you, such grand mysteries to share. What glories we will see, Richard! They defy all description!"

"That sounds delightful, aunt." I said this in complete ignorance of the mysteries and delights to which she referred. Possibly they were related to her big upcoming event, but what that might be I couldn't imagine.

"Yes, I think I will invite Wilus back, once the preparations are complete. There are services he can perform. Thank you for your candor with me, Richard. It's important that we are honest with one another, that we trust each other."

"That means a lot to me, too."

She smiled at me with deep affection and then blew a kiss my way, and magically, I felt it press against my brow, warm and tender, just as I remembered her kisses from childhood.

"So much still to do," she sighed in a distant manner, as if she were addressing someone else, and then she turned and strode away with her silk gown swishing noisily. I assumed she had retired to her bedroom, for I did not see her again during the next hour; but I was mistaken. We were to meet again later that same night.

Over the past few days, Julia (or should I say "Rebecca") had reconfigured the hidden room to the state it was in years ago when she had used it for her much-whispered-about meetings. I had gotten wind of this when I noticed her gathering chairs from all over the house and lugging them in the direction of the hidden room. That effort was followed by her breaking into the pantry early one morning and hauling all of her occult books back upstairs—to the hidden room, I assumed, where she no doubt returned them to the shelves. I had almost said something, had almost asked if I could help, but decided against it. The truth was, I was afraid of her, of what kind of creature she was, and what terrible things she planned to do up there, once she'd reassembled her cult.

A few minutes after eleven p.m., still believing Rebecca had long since gone to bed, I was passing through the hallway outside the bedroom that opens into the hidden room, when I saw a faint, flickering yellow light on the walls of the bedroom, as if candles were burning inside the bedroom, or perhaps even in the hidden room beyond. This by itself was strange enough, but I also distinctly heard many voices, both male and female, joined together in some kind of chanting. This was an astounding development. Had she already called together her followers, and were they meeting right now, at this very moment, in the restored chamber? I found this difficult to believe, especially as I hadn't noticed her making any phone calls yet, and hadn't detected any guests arriving during the evening. Yet the evidence presented to my senses was undeniable. Hell, I even smelled hot candle wax. I was certain she had somehow contacted everyone on her list and was now holding one of their ridiculous occult ceremonies, without telling me. But the timing was all wrong. Hadn't she promised to give me a role in the proceedings, and said that she would teach me all about the grand cosmic mysteries that had been revealed to her by that beastly deity—what was its name— Kamog? It made no sense.

My confusion was immediately supplanted by a more urgent concern, an intense fear that the careless and irrational "Julia" would accidentally set fire to the house. For although she spoke and felt emotionally like Rebecca, she looked like a cleaned-up version of the homeless wreck, Julia Spencer, and thus I thought of her as potentially behaving just as foolishly as Julia might. In a panic, I dashed through the bedroom and into the hidden room, only to find Julia—or was she Rebecca?— sitting alone in one of the chairs she'd recently placed there, in near total darkness, with the only illumination being the gentle moonlight that filtered through the chinks in the boards of the outer wall. She was—to my amazement—in the center of a circle of unlit candles.

"Ah, Richard—you're still up. You caught me here indulging myself in the pleasures of imagination, dreaming of the happiness that will soon be ours. I can almost hear their voices now, and feel the warmth of the glowing tapers. How lovely it will be on that glorious night! Can you bear to wait another day? I know I cannot. It's more thrilling than any film premiere could be. It will be the crowning achievement of my entire life."

"Ah … no, I can't wait either. I'm excited about it, for both of us. I can't imagine what it will be like."

"You'll know soon enough, dear. The time draws nigh. We must be patient."

"Right—patient. Well, goodnight, Aunt Rebecca. Sweet dreams."

She stared at me and smiled in a way I did not enjoy. "Sweet dreams, my dear," she whispered, and with that she closed her beautiful eyes, smiled, and returned to her unimaginable reverie. This odd encounter with Rebecca in the murky depths of the hidden room left me confused and conflicted. She still had about her an undeniable warmth, a sweet tenderness that remained despite her fundamental transformation from a living person into some bizarre and mysterious phantasm, an eerie recreation of her former self. The naked truth of the matter was that she was a disembodied spirit temporarily inhabiting the body of an unwilling host, the unfortunate and helpless Julia; and yet, somehow, she was still my beloved great-aunt, the same kind person who had tucked me in at night when as an innocent child I had feared the shadows lurking in the corners of my room. I did not know what to make of her, or how I should feel about her. My emotions were an uneasy mixture of outright horror and unconditional love, from which, regardless of the intolerable things she had done to Julia, I could not free myself. Wandering the hallways in a mental fog, preoccupied with these doubts, I found myself—without consciously intending it—headed for the small bedchamber where I had slept as a boy. The moonlight streaming in through the open window provided enough illumination that I didn't bother switching on the electric light, and after that weird scene with Rebecca, I wasn't in the right frame of mind for lighting the candle on the nightstand. With heavy weariness, I eased myself into a sitting position on the edge of the bed, placed my hands on the covers at either side of me, and stared at the empty wall across the room, the wall whereon, when I was a child, menacing shadows had so disturbed me. Vague shadows now played upon its surface in a watery and rippling fashion caused, no doubt, by the effects of moonbeams on the gauzy curtains that fluttered in the cool breeze. My mind was vacant, too overtaxed to form any more coherent thoughts. All I wanted was the solace and escape, the oblivion of sleep. I slowly turned to my right and saw what I knew would be there on the nightstand beside the unlit candle: the slender vial of greenish liquid—the elixir of dreams. Lying next to the bottle was the silver spoon with its curious handle ending in a key. Despite its age, the metal was still bright, devoid of the purple tarnish usually seen on old silver items.

Without giving it much thought, I picked up the slim bottle, gave it a brief shake, and poured a dose of the contents into the spoon's bowl. It looked slightly oily in the weak moonlight, the surface of the potion swirling with all the hues of a rainbow. I lifted the spoon to my lips and carefully dipped the tip of my tongue into the fluid to test it. It had the sweetish, licorice-like flavor I remembered. Then I quickly gulped down the rest before I could change my mind. Its warmth instantly spread throughout my chest.

I leaned back, sideways on the bed, and closed my eyes. In seconds, I was transported to a magical place: a lush but neatly-manicured park with broad green lawns carpeting rolling hills where dappled sunlight played between the trees as children ran in wild abandonment, squealing in delight. I was young, very young, and I yearned to join the other children in play, to follow wherever they might go. We were sitting a considerable distance from them, on a blanket my aunt had spread under one of the larger oaks. Aunt Rebecca was wearing the kind of knee-length plaid wool skirt that women wore in the 1960s.

"Can I go too?" I asked, a note of pleading in my voice.

"Not just yet, Richard. We need to talk."

"Talk? About what?" As if to put my mind at ease, she scooted over onto the blanket and put her arm around my shoulder. She planted a kiss on the side of my head and I smelled the wonderful fragrance of her hair.

"About you and your feelings."

"My feelings?"

"Yes. You've been troubled since I returned. Deeply troubled. You're even a little bit afraid of me, aren't you?"

I hung my head, ashamed of the truth.

"That's okay," she reassured me. "There's nothing wrong with that. It's a normal reaction to an unusual circumstance. Not many people have a loved one return from beyond death's door. That's one way to think of death, Richard: as a doorway, a passage into another, greater place. A golden realm of splendor and glory. We all go through that door eventually, but we still continue to exist in some other way. We still live, in a sense. Our thoughts and our feelings don't just stop when we die. Mine didn't. For example, I still love you, very much, and I still care about the things that were important to me during my life. Nothing much has changed, really. I'm just in a different place. Or, I was, until I found a way to come back to this world physically. I knew this was possible because I'd studied under some very knowledgeable people, the great poet Edward Derby and his lovely and brilliant wife, Asenath, and they taught me a method, a technique that provides a way to return. All it took was the right subject—well, the right person—to help me. That was Julia Spencer. Poor, misguided Julia. You're fond of her, aren't you?"

"Yes," I admitted, again feeling shame.

"There's nothing wrong with that. You have a good heart, a generous heart, and you see the good in everyone, even someone like Julia. It's not bad that you care about her, but you shouldn't let your concern for her welfare disturb you too much. After all, she's not exactly unhappy where she is now. In fact, she's quite content."

"Where is she?"

"Well, as I told you once before, she's in my tomb of stone, where I rest with my parents. She sleeps in the remains of the body I once wore when I was alive. She's not suffering, Richard. You needn't worry about Julia. She's fine."

"I don't?"

"No, you don't. You were worried about her, weren't you?"

"Yes," I said, my voice small and timid.

"Such a dear boy," she said, kissing me again, but this time her kiss quickly moved from my ear to my lips, and it became strange and exciting in a way that my childish mind did not understand, as if she were going to give me a silent message that made my little heart pound.

"I love you, Aunt Rebecca."

"I love you too, Richard. Now go and join the others. You still have time to catch up if you run fast. That's a good boy!"

The children were on the crest of a far-off hill, about to disappear over it to the other side. Even at this distance, I could hear the echoes of their gleeful voices. I broke away from my aunt's embrace, leaped up and ran as fast as I could towards the retreating children, but before I could reach them, they had crested the hill and were out of sight, although I could still hear them. When I reached the top myself, I saw them far below, racing into a shadowed valley that was wildly overgrown, and nothing like the park we had just left. I desperately ran down after the others, but as I penetrated more deeply into the valley, the lurid vegetation grew progressively thicker and became strewn with treacherous thorns, while the twisting path got steeper and was dangerously uneven, with jagged rocks jutting up everywhere. Halfway down the hill, I struck a rock, stumbled and lost my footing. At near-freefall speed, I began tumbling out of control into a jumbled, incoherent darkness—part wild valley, part emotional oblivion—that I instinctively knew held nothing for me but a brief moment of pain and loneliness, followed by endless nothingness. Deep,

deep down I fell, into a lost realm of eternal darkness. All of the children were gone, their voices suddenly muted, and I felt terribly abandoned.

When I briefly came to hours later, I felt calmer. The effects of the elixir had worn off, and normal consciousness had returned. Without fully awakening, I shambled down the hall and into my own room, where the bed was larger and I could spread out comfortably. I had no further dreams after that.

... a book in her lap, mumbling a song as she twined twigs and leaves into her hair.

CHAPTER NINE

I awoke to the sound of wind as it sang eerily in the tree outside my room's window. Something in the oddness of the noise lured me out of bed, and I moved to the window, knelt before it and rested my arms on its sill. As my senses became fully awake and aware, I realized that the singing was not the wind whispering through the tree limbs but came from below, near the bottom of the trunk; then I recognized whose voice it was that crooned, and I grabbed a jacket and rushed to the main floor and out the front door.

She sat upon the earth, her legs crossed, with a book in her lap, mumbling a song as she twined twigs and leaves into her hair.

"Aunt Rebecca?"

Her eyes met mine, and she shook her head. "Nar, she's sleeping. Can you smell the ointment she's put into my hair? What is that fragrance, lilacs or something? My hair is so soft from her brushing it." She held up a leaf to me. "It was homesick for its 'elements of earth.' That's one of her poems, you know." Julia nodded to the book in her lap, and I saw that it was Rebecca's *Step into the Moonlight, and Other Poems*. Her hands empty of twigs, Julia picked up the book and opened it, and then she began to recite.

"I bend in beams of moonlight to the ground
And claw into the elements of earth

81

To rummage for whatever might be found
Within the womb of squalid mortal birth;
For we are formed from elements of mud.
To muck and mire, in time, all is returned.
In time our liquid eyes, our bones and blood
Enjoy the rich corruption they have earned.
I claw into the elements of grime
And wash my face with hands that wear its stain,
And laugh into the element of time
That cannot hold me as I sink again
Into the blessed elements of death
To which I squander final mortal breath."

She dropped the book into her lap and dug both hands into the earth as she swayed her body back and forth. Again, she began to hum her eerie elegy. "Julia," I whispered; but she placed a soiled finger to my mouth and hushed me, and then she lifted her dark hands to my visage and began to rub filth into my flesh. "Where is Rebecca?"

"I told you, she's sleeping. But not in the element of earth, 'cos they put her in a stony box in a room of smooth marble. Aye, her quiet bed of rock." She nodded her head as she peered into my eyes. I placed my warm hands over her own. "She loves you—but *it* hates you."

"It?"

"The fiend that has corrupted her. The devil that will ultimately usurp us." Her voice took on an altered tone, the one with which she performed her poetry at readings. "But I do not mind; for I have dreamed of resting in eternal darkness, in that silent realm. It is a place beyond reach, into which the cruelty of men cannot find hold, for men have no desire for my discarded husk. Never again will hungry men lure me to their sinful lairs and do their dirty deeds. Nevermore will I taste that pain and ignominy. I will rest where men cannot ravage, and I will rot with the silent world. And *it* will murder time."

My flesh grew cold, as if encased in icy fever. What torments and abuses had this woman suffered? I wanted to embrace her, and yet I hesitated, for I was a man, of the race of brutes who had defiled her. She looked at me strangely and then pressed her stained hands to the tears that began to stream down my face. "I'm sorry," I muttered meekly.

She looked at me with a curious expression on her face, and then she moved her hands to her hair and removed one of the twigs therein. Reaching for me, she began to fasten the twig into my hair. "I think you're my friend," she whispered.

"I am your devoted friend," I assured her.

Beautifully, she smiled. "I've never had a friend before." She shut her eyes and rested her head against my shoulder; and then she shuddered, and I took her fully into my arms. I held her for a little while before her lips moved to my face and kissed my cheek, in a way that was familiar. "Richard, dear boy—how very noble of you."

Rebecca had returned.

CHAPTER TEN

I was in the kitchen scrambling eggs when Rebecca swept into the room, where she looked about high and low with obvious impatience. I didn't think she was up yet and was a bit disappointed to see her, as I had hoped to have an hour alone to enjoy a leisurely breakfast before I would have to deal with my aunt and the perplexing questions surrounding her present nature and motivations.

"What have you done with it, Richard?"

"With what, Auntie? And good morning, by the way."

"With the damn telephone, of course! It's supposed to be right here on the table beside the pantry door!" She stood with hands on hips, staring at the empty table as if she might force the phone to materialize through sheer willpower, and then rolled her head in an ever-widening circle, inspecting every portion of the room. Did she expect to see the device dangling from the ceiling above the cast-iron stove? Or, absurdly, find it tucked into the space behind the ancient icebox that I no longer used but kept out of sentiment? I couldn't imagine what she thought her frenzied searching would produce, other than annoyance for both of us.

"It's gone. We no longer have a land line. After I got the cell phone, I had the old telephone disconnected. It's in the attic if you want to see it, but the line is dead."

"You did *what*?"

She was outraged, and for a second I felt guilty for having made this change in her home, but—after all—she'd been dead a good while and I no longer used the old phone. It was a useless relic at that point.

"I had it disconnected. The line is no longer in service. Why pay for a land line when I do all of my business on the cell? It's a waste of money."

"Bah! Money is no concern of yours. I left you a bundle in the bank, dear nephew. You should not make decisions based merely on costs. We have a fine home and a reputation to maintain. What will our guests think when they see we have no telephone?"

"They all have cell phones now, too. They'll think nothing of it."

"Those stupid pieces of plastic are not really telephones. They're toys for the idiots who have become slaves to modern gadgets. Bah! Bring me my telephone at once."

At this point, I gave up trying to defend my actions. I scraped the cooked eggs onto a plate and then went up to the attic to fetch the old phone. It was one of those candlestick designs of the 1920s, a heavy instrument made of black Bakelite, where the mouthpiece hangs on a metal cradle extending from the top of the cylindrical "candlestick" base. The thing was lying where I'd left it, on top of a box of tattered Theosophy magazines that I had planned to donate to the library.

"Here it is," I said, returning a minute later, "although, honestly, I don't know what use it can be to you." My eggs were still warm, thankfully, and the coffee maker had just finished filling its carafe. Now all I needed was hot toast and real butter. "Care to join me? I made enough eggs for the two of us."

"No, thank you. I have calls to make." With this, she placed the telephone in the same position it had always held, in the center of the small table, on top of a dust-impregnated embroidered piece that long ago had covered a floor-model radio cabinet.

"It doesn't work anymore. You can't call out on that," I warned, knowing it was useless. She would do as she pleased.

"Preposterous." She picked up the telephone, held the speaker to her ear, and blew into the mouthpiece as if to clear away the intervening period since last she'd used it. "By the way, one of my books is missing. It wasn't in the pantry and I can't find it anywhere."

"Which one is that?" I asked, already guessing the title.

"It's called *INCANTATIONS OF KAMOG*, and it really is essential to our work."

Just as I suspected. "Oh, that book has suffered a mishap."

"What do you mean?"

"Exactly that. I was reading it in my bedroom one night, and in a moment of, well, impatience with the authors and their dreary insistence upon evil as the only thing worth pursuing in life—I threw it across the room. I'm afraid it didn't fare too well. The pages are all loose now, although I think I can get them back together again. It's in a binder sort of affair. The screw posts broke and it flew all apart when it hit the wall."

"Really, Richard. You must treat books with more respect. They're not gym equipment."

"I hope you aren't angry with me."

"No, certainly not; although I would like the book back regardless of its condition."

I finished chewing my eggs, took a quick sip of hot coffee, and then jumped up. "I'll fetch it for you. Give me a few minutes to put it back together."

"No hurry, dear child."

The damned Kamog book was where I'd left it, concealed in the drawer of my nightstand. Collating the pages back into order took longer than it should have. As for the binding, the screw posts were hopelessly ruined in the collision with the wall, but I thought I could replace them with a pair of long bootlaces that would hold the book together well enough. Using a tapestry needle, I pulled the laces through the holes in the stack of pages and the leatherette covers, and then tied them off in knots. The resulting "binding" was sloppy, and not as good as the binder posts had been, but at least the book was serviceable again, even though it was still an abomination. My opinion of its value hadn't altered.

By the time I was done with the repair job, forty-five minutes had passed. Proud of my handiwork, I brought the book down to the kitchen to show Rebecca.

She was sitting at the table, her contact lists spread out everywhere except where my dirty plate and cup still sat, and speaking to someone on the visibly disconnected telephone, its cut wires trailing in the air. This was weird enough—but stranger still was that someone was *listening* on the other end of the line. Rebecca was saying "the time is nigh, the cycle has come full circle, and we must gather for the ultimate rite," or words to that effect. Every few seconds I heard the small, tinny sound of a distant voice answering her with short, unintelligible utterances. My aunt had no need of the phone company. Her occult willpower was that potent.

Without interrupting her conversation, I quietly laid the repaired book on the table and left her to her work.

"So I'll see you then?" she spoke into the mouthpiece.

There was a shrill reply that sounded like "Yes, I'll be there."

"Excellent. Good day to you, Wilus. Oh, and one more thing. Do bring that young Abraham Waite fellow, will you? He may have something to contribute. You're entirely welcome. Goodbye."

Turning to me she explained, "I'm inviting them all to the ceremony tonight. You'll be there too. May I count on your assistance?"

I felt a sudden uneasiness in the pit of my stomach, anxiety at having my privacy assaulted by a big social event in the house, perhaps, but I ignored it. "Sure. I wouldn't miss it."

"That's a good boy." She then dialed the next number on her list and began speaking into the mouthpiece again.

CHAPTER ELEVEN

Rebecca was on the telephone all morning, dialing her contacts and then, once she'd worked her way through the entire list and checked off each name, going back to the start of the list and calling them all back at least once, if not several times. "Rebecca Pascal here. One more thing …" she would begin loudly, and then her voice would drop to a secretive whisper and I could never quite make out what she was telling them. I gathered from her tone that she was priming them with challenging new ideas, giving them "homework" assignments, or in some cases asking probing questions of those about whose loyalty and dedication she had doubts—all designed to ensure the success of the coming ceremony. Despite having promised several times to teach me about her occult beliefs and practices, so far she had made no attempt to do so, for which I was quietly grateful. I didn't want to be instructed in her shadowy mystery religion, whatever it was, and had no desire to become familiar with the contemptible beast she and her followers worshiped, that fiendish Kamog creature. Maybe she meant for me to learn through observation, a sort of "on-the-job" training, just by being present at the ritual and participating in whatever it was she and the cultists would be doing tonight. I certainly wasn't about to ask her to begin teaching me. Thankfully, she was preoccupied with her voodoo phone conversations. By early afternoon I was feeling antsy. I needed to get out of the house and started looking for an excuse to leave. Checking the refrigerator and the pantry, I saw that we were low on staples, having nothing in the way of refreshments to serve our guests. No snacks, no munchies, no wine or beer or even soda.

"Pardon me, Auntie," I said loudly enough to get her attention. "I'm going to the store to pick up some refreshments for tonight. Do you need anything? Any special requests?"

"That's a good idea, dear," she said, distractedly waving me away. "Whatever you think appropriate."

It was good to get outside, away from the freakish and unnatural situation at home. Driving to the grocery store down the tree-lined streets of Arkham, the sun warm at my back, the radio playing a familiar pop tune, felt wonderfully normal and peaceful. Once at the store, I lingered far longer than necessary, piling my cart high with a vast array of delectable foods and beverages. Platters of cut veggies, several kinds of dips, a tray of cold cuts from the deli counter, six bottles of wine—three whites, three reds—and four six-packs of locally brewed craft beer. The tab came to almost $200. Back when I had been a working stiff, before receiving my inheritance, the amount would have been daunting to me. Now, handing the clerk my debit card, I thought nothing of it. I loaded everything into the trunk of the car and pulled out of the parking lot, but I wasn't ready to return home yet. It was a mild day, and I figured everything would keep for a while and there was no need to rush back to Rebecca and her interminable conversations. Hardly knowing where I was going, I found myself driving across town in the direction of Hangman's Hill and, eventually, the Old Wooded Graveyard. I gradually realized that I intended to pay Julia a visit, asleep in Rebecca's corpse. That's where Rebecca had said poor Julia was, and I took her at her word. I wanted to see her for myself, to gaze at her— or rather, at Rebecca's cadaver which supposedly housed Julia's slumbering spirit, and see if I could detect the homeless poet's presence, and even judge her state of mind. Was she content, dreaming peacefully, as Rebecca claimed? Or was she an unhappy prisoner, trapped against her will in the decaying remains of a dead woman? I would see with my own eyes. I parked the car and locked it, for there were reports of thieves and worse in the vicinity of the graveyard. No one seemed to be about, lending the burial grounds a quiet melancholy, but the day was nonetheless pleasant, and in the golden afternoon light it was possible to not be afraid, to actually enjoy the gloomy atmosphere of the place. A brief wandering through the overgrown grounds brought me to the inclined ground on which Rebecca's opulent tomb had been erected. It shouldn't have startled me to find the huge stone doors ajar, and to spy the chain and iron lock that had previously secured the doors lying discarded nearby, for the last time I'd been at the site I had watched Lorne and his band of delinquents as they clustered rowdily about the tomb, doing God knows what sorts of childish vandalism to the family sepulcher and its fittings. I stooped and picked up the lock at my feet, the iron of which was cold with the chill of hard-packed dirt. The lock had been cut with bolt cutters, for which I blamed—without justification— Abraham Waite.

Dropping the damaged lock, I swung one of the doors further on its squealing iron hinges until the gap between the doors was wide enough for me to enter. The air of the tomb was stale and chilly, the inside light quite dim. Searching about, I found a wooden torch set into a holder on the wall near the entrance. It had been wrapped in a coarse fabric that was soaked in some flammable material, most likely pitch. When I touched my pocket lighter to it, the torch head burst into bright yellow flame, providing adequate illumination for further exploration. It didn't take me long to orient myself. The ground floor of the mausoleum consisted of a large, disturbingly plain chamber, at the center of which was located a narrow stone stairway that led precipitously down to an equally narrow hallway that branched out into a series of underground crypts. Something about the dimensions and proportions of the cheerless stonework reminded me of the old black-and-white photos I'd seen of the tombs of Egyptian kings. The only décor seemed to be some shallow bas-relief panels chiseled along the walls at about waist-height that depicted sad cherubim, colonial-style skulls and crossbones, and other grim reminders of humanity's mortality. Several minutes of wandering these dark recesses convinced me that all of the crypts but one were completely empty. That single occupied crypt held the vaults of Rebecca and her parents. Presumably the other crypts patiently awaited the day they would hold the rest of her family members, relatives who were still, at present, alive—including (wretched thought) myself.

The burial vaults of Rebecca and her parents were all of recent manufacture, for she had arranged to have her parents' bodies exhumed from their prior humble plots and moved to her more stately new mausoleum not long before her own death. Thus, the vaults did not show an undue amount of deterioration or encrustation such as might be seen in a typical tomb where the contents have lain undisturbed by anyone but rats for decades or even centuries. The copper nameplates were still mostly bright red, although a greenish verdigris was beginning to form on Rebecca's alone. A thin veil of cobwebs was the sole marker of Time's passing upon the parental vaults, and—as I expected—their vault lids were still snugly in place, not having been touched since the day of their re-interment. Rebecca's burial vault was another matter. It was more heavily draped with gauzy webs, and its massive lid—which was shockingly dislodged—bore a thick layer of white bird droppings, no doubt thanks to the mausoleum doors having been left unsecured and the tomb exposed to the elements.

Who had been here, and who had dared to unseal her vault? I instinctively assigned responsibility to Wilus Lorne and his debauched crew. Obviously, they had returned at some point after our last joint visit here and dabbled obscenely and indecorously with Rebecca's remains. The fiends!

With considerable effort, I was able to slide the already-dislodged vault lid several more inches to the right, further exposing the coffin inside, but the lid was still in the way, blocking my access to the coffin. And the coffin was my goal, for I wished to gaze upon the face of Rebecca's decaying corpse and witness for myself Julia's current state of being. If I could slide the vault lid just a couple inches more to the right, it would no longer obstruct my prying open the separately-hinged lid at the head of the casket. The vault lid was very weighty and resisted any movement. As out of shape as I was, it took all of my physical strength to budge it again, but when it did move, it shifted much more to the right than I intended, and to my shock, the stubborn stone lid slid entirely off the top of the burial vault and came crashing to the floor, missing my feet by inches. I was very lucky it didn't land on my foot, for it would certainly have broken the foot and may have trapped me there indefinitely—a horrifying thought.

Now the top of the coffin was entirely exposed. I tugged at the edge of the lid and it lifted easily, but I stopped there, hesitating. Did I really want to see Rebecca's corpse? What an alarming idea! I had no illusions; I knew that she would look bad, very bad, but wasn't it terrible enough to merely imagine what that might look like? Surely, it would be a mistake to burn the actual image into my brain forever. I waited ... not lowering the lid back down, not raising it all the way up ... holding my breath, painfully aware that I was lingering foolishly in a shadowy crypt below ground, in an abandoned tomb, in ghoul-haunted Arkham. This was madness, and yet I continued waiting. A sudden clattering sound to my left made me jump, but I did not let go of the coffin lid.

Surely it was some restless rat, scurrying along the base of the crypt wall, searching for something corrupt on which it could gnaw. Finally exhaling, I rapidly drew a fresh breath (if tomb air can ever be called fresh) and with sudden determination yanked high the coffin lid so as to reveal my great-aunt's face in death.

Nothing could have prepared me for what met my eyes.

I had expected her to look very aged, deeply wrinkled, her skin tone pale, waxen even, perhaps with some sinking, some collapsing of the flesh as the body dried out.

What I saw was a horror, an abomination suitable only for a demented house of freaks or a hellish carnival sideshow. A gnarled skeleton clothed in stretched and cracked and yellowed parchment, its jaws yawning wide, the lips long since withered away and the bared teeth—fang-like in their jawbone sockets—grinning with unholy, nightmarish glee. Nothing could have been worse than the thing I looked upon. It was intolerable, far beyond my most gruesome fears. And yet, I kept the coffin lid up and stared senselessly at her awful physiognomy. If I waited long enough, I prayed, I might ultimately see past this vile ruin of what had once been a human form, might peer deeply enough into and through the stinking mass of desiccated tissues to detect the presence of Julia's spirit.

I saw nothing but Rebecca's dead carcass in all of its absurd grotesquerie. There was no sign of Julia Spencer to be seen. She was not present.

I would give it one minute more, and then I would leave this appalling place. I literally counted down the seconds—"thousand one … thousand two … thousand three …"—feeling childish as I did so.

At "thousand forty-five," about to give up, I heard a sound. Clearly not a scampering rat, nor a stray sparrow. It was faint, thin and distant, and yet it clearly came from the coffin. It sounded like someone singing. A woman's voice, gentle and peaceful, as though she were humming a wordless hymn or a sweet nursery rhyme tune. And it was definitely Julia's voice.

I'm ashamed to confess that in terror I dropped the coffin lid, grasped the torch from where it lay flickering against the wall, scrambled madly up the dusty stone steps and hastily fled the tomb, neglecting to close the stone doors behind me, not bothering to weave the chain through the door handles or to hang the broken lock in its rightful place.

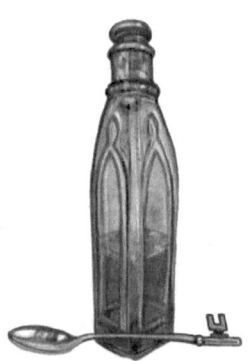

CHAPTER TWELVE

When I returned home I busied myself with putting away the groceries. I had no idea how long I had been away from the house, and I feared my prolonged absence might have displeased my aunt, whom I was anxious to avoid. Quietly, I left the kitchen and went to the stairs, determined to return to my room; but as I began to climb the stairs a voice called to me from the living room. Sighing, I walked into the room, where all the lights were out, the one illumination being from the fire in the hearth. Flickering shadows played along the figure of my aunt, who sat in her armchair next to the fireplace, a book in her lap. I did not have to see the book clearly to know that it was *INCANTATIONS OF KAMOG*.

Rebecca's eyes shimmered, reflecting firelight. She frowned and said, "You reek of death, Richard. Your eyes have been affected and wear a haunted hue. Where have you been?"

"I went shopping. You don't have any lights on. You can't read in the dark."

She chuckled. "Do you know, such is the power of this text that I no longer need to read it to *absorb* it." Opening the book, she ran her fingers along one page, as if she were a blind woman reading by Braille. "I drink it in, and it nourishes my soul, and feeds my brain. It's outré how I can sense a text beneath the printed words, one that teaches the occult things of which it is comprised. I've learned, tonight, a remarkable new trick. I can, with keen concentration, subdue more than one soul at a time. My hold on this second soul isn't as potent as my hold on the other, but with time my knack will strengthen."

I felt a sudden fit of annoyance that was close to anger. "And what's the point of all of this? How can it possibly profit you?"

Her mouth curled into such a curious smile, and she shook slightly, as if consumed with sardonic mirth. "It's frightfully amusing, for one thing. But there is more. A daemonic flame flares within me, and it is called Kamog. It pines to stretch from out its lunatic dimension and slink into our own, for it has a longing for mortal carnage. The smell of human blood, Richard, is a powerful intoxicant. One has only to read your Old Testament to see the allure of blood. It was blood painted onto doorways that caused the Angel of Death to pass certain houses. It was the blood of sacrifice that was sprinkled onto altars of God, and its stench was sweet unto the Lord. Oh, pretty stench of slain mortality!"

I watched as she lifted one hand to her face and pierced her flesh with a sharp fingernail. The thin line of liquid that slipped down her countenance looked black in the darkened room. I watched that tiny liquid stream as it caught firelight, and I imagined that I could smell it, too; and the power of that fragrance so overwhelmed me that I fell on my knees before the hearth.

The woman in the chair cocked her head at me and smiled. "Come lick my wound, my pet."

"No."

"Really? Then allow me to show you my new trick. It may amuse you."

Although the fire beside me was hot, I shivered at the tone of her voice. I wanted to take my eyes away from hers but could not. Then my brain began to freeze with numbing pain, and my eyesight blurred. I groaned as I lifted my hands to my aching head so as to caress it. I moaned, and then my voice detached itself from me, and I knew that I was losing my hold on sanity as I began to see *through* my hands. Those hands melted from view, and I sat in the armchair nodding to the one who knelt before me. I watched him lower his hands from before his face— *my* face—and after a moment's pause I saw him smile. He crept to the chair in which I sat and pressed his lips to the blood that stained my visage. Shutting my eyes, I moaned once more, as his smooth wet tongue moved over me, and then he kissed me, and my brain was suddenly free of its chilliness. I took my face away from the woman before whom I knelt, and swallowed the taste of her blood that was on my tongue.

She gazed at me for a long silent moment. "Your eyes have retained the reflection of my corpse upon their surface—your haunted eyes." She sniffed. "The rot of my carcass still lingers in your hair. What a paltry thing, mortality. You will be happy when I free you from it and number you among mine own." A knock sounded on the front door. "Ah, our company has arrived. Do let them in, dear nephew."

CHAPTER THIRTEEN

I heard a great many footsteps shuffling on the porch just beyond the front door, and the electric bell was ringing impatiently. This should have come as no surprise, timed as it was in conjunction with my aunt's announcement that our guests were beginning to arrive, and yet it startled me. Playfully, she pushed at me with one foot, and I rose off my knees. Defensively, I peeked around the edge of the curtains. What I saw was a veritable herd of figures filling the porch, with others coming up the steps and still more filing along the walkway from the street. And out on the street, several automobiles—some of them quite ancient— were parked, their passengers emerging, while other vehicles idled in the road, their drivers searching for a parking space.

"Don't just stand there like an idiot, silly boy! Open the door!"

I flinched at the harshness in her tone. "Of course; sorry." Taking a deep breath, I went to the door and opened it. An elderly couple dressed in vintage finery stared at me with an unconcealed hesitancy in their eyes that bordered on suspicion.

"Master Richard?" asked the gentleman. He was around the same age Rebecca would have been had she still lived, and yet he seemed much older.

"Yes. I'm Rebecca's great-nephew. I live here now, since my aunt ... um ... well ... Please, do come in." I ushered them in, and would have asked if I could take their coats or if they cared for refreshments, but Rebecca had already raced to the door from out of the shadows and was warmly greeting them, so I turned to the next pair of guests, a well-dressed middle-aged couple. "Hello, I'm Richard Pascal. I don't think we've met."

"Mister and Missus Jenkins. So nice to finally meet you, Richard. Rebecca has told us so much about you."

And thus it went until the last guest had been greeted and the room was filled to standing-room-only density. Among the guests were many I did not recognize, and a few I did, including Wilus Lorne and his gaggle of black-clad occultists, among whom was the young hooligan, Abraham Waite. The majority of the guests were older and obviously affluent, and from their comments I gathered they had been followers and associates of my aunt's back in the days when her "study group"—as she laughingly called it— was active. The scattering of younger people, other than Lorne's party, seemed to be individuals Rebecca had recently attracted since her return to the house. How she had managed to reach out to such strangers and recruit them to her cause was a mystery.

Standing out distinctly from all of these relatively normal people was one couple who struck me as being very eccentric, to the degree of freakishness. This bizarre pair, a man and woman judging from their shabby attire, were so completely covered in clothing from head to foot that almost no portion of their skin could be seen. Gloves hid their hands, while scarves concealed their necks and hats obscured their hair. Both wore sunglasses, which was odd considering the fact that the sun had been down for over an hour. Accentuating their unusual demeanor was the strange fragrance they gave off as they shambled past me and into the house. While they had attempted to mask it with perfumes and cologne, the underlying odor was so pungent it came through in spite of their efforts, and its absolutely foul nature was unmistakable. They had a stench of rotting flesh about them that immediately brought back horrific images of my visit to the tomb that very afternoon.

"Richard, do be a dear and see about the refreshments, will you?"

"First I'll put on the lights," I suggested, moving towards the wall switch. It seemed ridiculous that the guests could see one another only as silhouettes against the flickering glow of the fireplace.

"No, Richard—please don't."

"But ..."

"Trust me. I have my reasons. I want everyone's pupils fully dilated, their night vision at its keenest. You'll see why in a moment."

"Not even a few candles?"

"No, not even candles for a while."

"Okay," I sighed, resigning myself to going along with her odd whims.

The kitchen felt unusually cheery with all of its lights ablaze. At moments like this, I realized we needed some help around the house. Having a maid to tend to domestic tasks would free me up to mingle with our guests instead of being stuck in the kitchen frantically preparing the snacks. We certainly could afford it. I filled two trays with cold cuts, chips, dips and such, and opened several bottles of wine. Returning to the party, I took care not to trip in the dark, setting the trays on a table by the hearth and then returning to the kitchen for the wine and glasses.

Rebecca called me over with a wiggling gesture of her finger. When I was near, she put her lips to my ear and whispered: "Did you see them? There are two here who were not invited ... not by me, at least."

"I invited no one," I whispered back. "What do you mean?"

"Surely you noticed the overdressed couple in sunglasses?"

"I did. And smelled them."

"Aha! Very good, Richard! You're learning. They have the stink of the grave about them. I sniffed them out the moment they stepped from their car."

"Who—or *what*—in heaven's name are they?"

"I'm not sure, but I sense they're here on some mission, acting on an enemy's behalf. I pissed off a lot of people in my time, Richard. Keep a close eye on them and don't let them out of your sight. And it wouldn't hurt to alert Wilus and his associates to the threat these interlopers present. If action is needed, who better to perform it than those healthy young men rippling with muscles? Of course, they must promise to maintain the strictest confidentiality in this matter. We don't want any hasty accusations being made."

"I'll talk to Lorne."

"That's a good lad," she said, patting me affectionately on the shoulder. Then she broke into uproarious laughter at a joke told by the well-heeled geezer beside her.

It was no easy task finding Lorne in the dark, and when I did, dragging him off to a corner for a quick powwow. Once he understood the situation, he seemed genuinely touched that Rebecca and I had taken him into our confidence, and he promised to muster the occultists to act as security against whatever disruption our uninvited guests might be plotting.

"It may be nothing," I mused.

"Better safe than sorry."

Rebecca began addressing the group while Lorne and I were concluding our exchange, and I missed her opening remarks. Everyone in attendance listened to her intently. As always, she had a commanding presence, which she used to full effect.

"And so," she concluded, "if you'll all kindly follow me through these double doors and out onto the patio, you'll witness a miraculous sight. Something for which we've all been waiting an interminable time."

106

"Hear, hear!" and "Brava!" some guests called out.

Thanks to a clear sky and the resulting unobstructed starlight, it was brighter outside than it had been in the house, and as guests filed by me, I saw many of them carrying books under their arms or in their hands. Most of the volumes looked like old religious or metaphysical texts, while a few followers held what were obviously their personal copies of Rebecca's book of poetry. Bookmarks and papers were inserted into most of these volumes, while some acolytes had a finger positioned at the page they wished to mark.

The sky was remarkably beautiful that night. It was as if the vast reaches of space were massive chambers in a celestial palace, subtly illuminated from unknown sources with infinitely graduated hues of light. The effect was one of great depth—depth beyond all human comprehension—creating the impression that every region gave onto yet another, more remote realm in an endless series of gargantuan anterooms and extended great halls. The crowd literally gasped when they saw this ethereal display in the heavens.

"Beautiful, indeed. But continue to watch, and a grand miracle you will see. The time draws nigh, my children. We gather on this appointed evening, this long-awaited night, at the end of a protracted cycle, to witness the arrival of Astarte, the goddess they call 'Abomination.' And it is She who with her eternal powers will burst open the gates for our beloved Kamog, for He strains against His shackles in the nether world, hungry for the blood of Earth's creatures, the nectar of their sticky souls!"

With those words, one particular star in the stunning celestial vault suddenly pulsed brightly as a welder's arc. It grew in size and brilliance until it filled a vast region in the nebular reaches. Beams of every color flashed from the star, while gobs of molten star matter seemed to bubble and drip from it. All about me, Rebecca's followers were mumbling, chanting, their books

It grew in size and brilliance until it filled a vast region in the nebular reaches.

open before them, their eyes darting from page to sky and back to page. Something about the situation terrified me, and I reeled in dizziness. Feeling I was about to faint, I grasped at the back of a steel patio chair for support.

"Shine down upon us, Ye Goddess of the Ethers! Bring Him forth unto this world of flesh and corruption, unleash Him upon us without mercy, we beseech thee! We welcome His killing embrace!" screamed Rebecca, falling to her knees upon the bricks, her hands clasped to her temples in an exaggerated show of ecstasy.

Several of the acolytes were beginning to howl at the pulsing star in the West. It seemed to beckon to them, to call them to a spot atop Hangman's Hill, above which it ceaselessly throbbed. That's when the vile deed Rebecca had foreseen transpired. It went down so fast that it was over with before I could make sense of what I was seeing.

The two uninvited beings simultaneously opened their coats to reveal to any whose gaze chanced to be fixed on them a pair of long ceremonial silver daggers clutched in gloved paws. In unison, they lunged murderously at Rebecca, bringing down the knives in sweeping arcs whose ultimate goal was to fatally pierce her bosom. My only reaction to this awful sight was one of intense, crippling fear and prospective grief for my beloved aunt and the severe harm that was about to be done to her.

Luckily, cooler minds prevailed. Instantly, the four nearest of the black-clad occultists sprang into action, tackling the would-be assassins and slamming them down against the patio bricks before they could fulfill their sinister mission. Most unexpected was the decisive action of young Abraham Waite; for while his companions held down the offending pair, Waite wrestled the dagger away from one of the fiends and tossed it aside. Then he pulled from within his shirt an antique gold medallion hanging on a heavy chain about his neck, pressed the thick relic flat against the creature's face, and spoke loudly in a powerful voice a series of ominous sounding words in an unknown language. The effect of this apparent magick was that it completely disabled and tormented the creature, who expressed his displeasure in agonized yowls and screeches followed by coughing, gasping, and croaking noises that I took for pleas of mercy. But Waite did not show him any mercy, and only pressed the golden medallion deeper into the thing's decaying flesh. When after a minute of this torture the hellish being expired, Waite attacked the other now-disarmed and fully restrained being in a similar fashion, killing her as well while his companions held her down, ignoring the thing's desperate bid for clemency. The crowd seemed both stunned and grateful for the finality of Waite's response. The bodies of these baleful entities—whom all present now realized had been dead for some time prior to that evening—immediately collapsed into putrescence and then rapidly deteriorated into a fine gray ash, which a sudden chilly breeze dissipated, until all that remained of the two were the piles of their pathetic rags.

Rebecca, momentarily stunned by the attack, rose unsteadily to her feet, uncharacteristically silent, but she quickly regained her composure.

"No, my children, I'm afraid there is no 'Balm in Gilead' for the likes of these! Sorry, Mr. Poe! There are those who oppose what we are about to do, but they are doomed to failure. Especially when we have such capable persons as Abraham Waite on our side. Thank you, sir."

I was flabbergasted, as my maternal grandsire used to say. Numb to what I'd just witnessed. Not knowing what to say, I kept silent and went about my business.

As instructed earlier by Rebecca, I handed a lit candle to each acolyte as they passed by me on their way back inside the house. Handing out the last candle, I fell in line at the end of the procession. The trek up the stairs and down the lengthy hall to the hidden room was made in eerie silence. None of the participants spoke. The only sound to be heard was that of many feet pressing upon the boards of the stairs and the soles of shoes brushing on the hallway carpets. The room was packed by the time I entered, but Rebecca urged me to stand beside her for the ceremony.

"Don't be shy, Richard. You have much to contribute."

Waite was already there, standing in the most favored position, on Rebecca's right. I was to take a somewhat less honored position to her left. I felt a bit miffed at this, but then again, he had performed admirably in foiling the attack.

Embarrassed at my relative demotion in her esteem, I squeezed my way through the throng until I reached the center of the circle, and took my spot beside my great-aunt. With all the candles burning, the room was well-lit and its air rich with the aroma of hot wax. At first I was anxious about what might happen next—for Rebecca had never taken the time to fully explain the ritual to me—but after a while a luxurious peacefulness overcame me, which was a welcome change from the terror of the attack and its shocking aftermath, just minutes before.

I decided to forget about the indignity of playing second fiddle to Waite and the loss of status thus implied. At least I was present, welcome here among Rebecca's friends and followers. It meant something that she cared enough to include me in this, the paramount event in her life—or, rather, afterlife.

Rebecca opened her copy of *INCANTATIONS OF KAMOG*—the copy I'd mended—and began to recite from one of the more lyrical passages. Her gaze remained on the celebrants surrounding her, and she never once looked down at the page, for she knew the selection by heart. In the golden glow of the candles, I noticed how beautiful she—or, rather, Julia's body—looked. But beyond that merely physical feminine beauty there was an inner radiance to her that was irresistible. No wonder she had been a film star. Even now, in this deplorable condition, she was celestial in her loveliness.

My fantastic aunt recited for what must have been a full ten minutes, but it seemed both to be over in seconds and to go on for hours. Her voice was perfect that night, flawless, as she delivered the words she knew by heart, and whose power she absorbed from the pages of the book through the tips of her slender fingers.

Rebecca's impassioned recitation and the rhythmically chanted responses of the group had a profound hypnotic effect on me. At some point I stopped hearing the literal words, so caught up was I in the heady, mounting psychic energy in the room. I understood that we were of one spirit, not separate and isolated souls, and that none of us need be lonely or sad ever again. Time itself stopped, and space ceased to exist. The night stretched out endlessly before us, an infinity of vibrant, eternal being. There was no death, no suffering, no misery—those were all mere illusions, the foolish fantasies of mortal brutes and boors. All that *really* existed in the infinite Now was the beating of countless hearts, the unlimited flowing of hot blood, the sweet tang of universal carnage. And then, with sudden excitement, without quite realizing just what was transpiring, we were migrating *en masse* down the stairs, pouring out of the doors of the house and into the wild night, and marching somnambulant and herd-like across Arkham—hell-bound for Hangman's Hill.

CHAPTER FOURTEEN

Witnesses to our strange procession across Arkham that night later reported that we were a most unusual sight, such as has never been seen before, even in the history of this ancient metropolis whose reputation has been beset by rumors of witchery since its founding. Although some few of us allegedly chanted or sang softly, the vast majority walked in eerie silence, a long column of uncanny figures shambling trance-like down the leaf-blown sidewalks, oblivious to our surroundings, with only one goal in mind—the hilltop graveyard that overlooks the city, where the worm-gnawed dead are said to keep a slumbering watch over the living denizens below.

I rely on these secondhand reports because I—like many another who was party to that march—remember very little of the actual walk across town. We were in a frenzied state of mind; indeed, in an altered state of consciousness. I do retain a fleeting recollection of seeing the Hobo Bean Coffee Company over on our left as we progressed along Church Street on our way from French Hill towards western Arkham. And after that, another fragmentary image resides in memory: the silhouette of the dark campus looming from the Arkham skyline, also on our left, as we passed Miskatonic University a couple of blocks later. Once we cleared Miskatonic (and I do not recall this part), another block brought us to Boundary Street, which we crossed and then entered the road up to Hangman's Hill.

Astronomers at Miskatonic's Science Department have gone on record as stating there were no unusual celestial phenomena occurring in the heavens that night, and certainly no reports were made—outside the claims of our little group—that an unexplainable aerial event was observed anywhere within the city. But we know what we saw: the brilliant, pulsating and dripping Astarte virtually marking the way for our caravan. It seemingly hung directly over the Old Wooded Graveyard in the northern sector of Hangman's Hill, and none of us will ever forget the moment when, halfway up the hill, we saw a vivid purple beam of light shoot down from the bewitched star, illuminating the very spot where Rebecca's mausoleum stood. Many a gasp and sigh rose from our throats, and our hearts beat wildly at the thrill of Her beckoning, for Astarte was now actively directing our troop forward, unmistakably revealing the Path to our fated rendezvous with the beast, Kamog.

The time between that remarkable vision and our arrival at the tomb is another blank in my memory. My next conscious recollection is that of standing among the throng of followers, listening intently as Rebecca continued the impassioned recitations from *INCANTATIONS OF KAMOG* that she had begun in the hidden room. Clustered tightly about her was Wilus Lorne and his band of black-clad occultists. At Rebecca's right stood Abraham Waite in all his newfound glory, with one hand presumptuously placed on her shoulder in imitation of a loving nephew (damn him!) and the other holding open the book of Kamog readings, but his role in this reading was merely a symbolic gesture, for she did not need to see the text physically, and Waite knew this as well as I did.

Her incantations went on for quite some time, the enthusiasm of Rebecca's followers building until it reached a nearly orgasmic state of excitement. Something about the soothing, comforting, persuasive tone of her voice was so compelling to them they were powerless to resist her every suggestion and command. In my hurt pride that she obviously favored Waite over me, I held back a bit from immersing myself in the ritual, and although I was deeply affected by the events unfolding around me, I was not completely under Rebecca's spell as were the rest of them.

Then, at what proved to be a critical point, Rebecca spoke a few words to us *ex tempore*—softly issued utterances that conveyed tender emotion—and took from Waite a slender volume which he presented her, a copy of her book of poetry. She opened it to what I later realized was page 58/59, the same leaf Waite had stolen from the Miskatonic University Library copy, and read the verse that many decades earlier she had written specifically for use at this moment: "Arise into the Air Ye Seekers and Join the Living Spirit"—the lyric that she always insisted would call down the terrible Kamog.

As she read, I noticed a disheveled figure lurking on the fringes of our assembly. The person remained in shadow, out of the circle of purple light, not wishing to be observed. Who might this be, I wondered? It was clearly not any of the guests I'd greeted at the house earlier. Fearing another would-be assassin, with great caution I inched closer to the lone figure until I was no more than fifteen feet away from it. Someone in rags. A bag of bones with yellowed skin, swathed in the tatters of a shredded silk evening gown.

My god!—it was Julia, lodged in Rebecca's corpse! Somehow she had sensed our presence and roused herself from her earthy dreams enough to form the desire to join us. And somehow she had mustered the strength of will to push up the unsealed lid and climb out of the coffin, and then to drag Rebecca's decayed bodily remains up those dark, lonesome stairs, out through the unchained doors of the tomb, and across an expanse of graveyard to this final position where even now she struggled to remain upright.

I was now quite a distance from the others, and out of range of their hearing as I whispered, "Julia! What on earth?"

She held a bony finger to her skeletal maw and with great effort croaked out quietly, so none but me would receive her words, "Nar, Master Richard. Please don't expose me. I've waited long for this, just like Wilus. Don't tell!"

"I won't. You have just as much right to be here as any of them, and more than Mr. Waite has. Your secret is safe." But did I really think Rebecca didn't know about Julia's presence? Nothing escaped Rebecca, and I was convinced she knew of Julia's proximity and, for some reason, tolerated it.

What next ensued was madness incarnate. I can only describe it as an unimaginably frightful storm that broke loose just as the last words of the poem fell from Rebecca's lips. I was later told by one of the attendees that what we experienced was the "opening of the Gate" by Astarte. I saw no gate, but the sky did seem to crack open all around the pulsing star, and behind it—if such a thing is possible—lay a domain of absolute blackness beyond all comprehension. Not merely material darkness, the complete want of light, but the absence of all matter, energy, being, spirit, time, space and anything else you could name or that exists but remains nameless. It was the Eternal Void itself.

From this unthinkably hideous realm, Kamog entered our world.

My vision could not process the scene before me, but my other senses told me that we were bathed in heat and coldness at the same time, and were under the influence of a powerful electrical field. Ozone burned my nostrils and the hair of my arms and neck literally stood on end.

All around me people were shrieking in abject terror. It was a while before I realized I myself was screaming in dread at what I felt approaching.

I never actually saw Kamog. I couldn't tell you what physical form he took, or if he had a face or other identifiable features. I sensed his fearsome presence, undeniably, and I will never fully recover from that mortal shock.

There's a rumor making the rounds in Arkham that Kamog resembled some gigantic Leviathan of the deep, but it doesn't seem to have its origins in any reputable source, and I don't give it credence.

What I did see was exactly what I reported to the skeptical police detectives. I described it to them as the bodily "ascension" of my beloved Aunt Rebecca—still occupying Julia's living body—along with Wilus Lorne and Abraham Waite. The three of them levitated (the detectives scoffed at this term, but what else can I call it?) high in the air above the tomb, while I and the others below looked on in horror and awestruck wonder. They hung there in mid-air, miraculously suspended, for what seemed like several minutes, slowly twisting and turning, revolving first clockwise and then counter-clockwise, back and forth like that … just *hanging* there.

That's when I began to truly fear for their safety.

I am told by the same individual (he wishes to remain anonymous to the public, and I honor that request) that Kamog then materialized to selected acolytes, my informant being one of these, and that he was "huge and monstrous." But those are relative terms, and the unnamed gentleman refused to elaborate further.

As the black-clad occultists chanted and wailed in greedy supplication to Kamog, I am told the beast reached down—for he apparently towered above even the levitated trio—and ripped the souls out of Rebecca, Lorne and Waite. "Ripped from their bodies" was the way I heard it expressed. I did not see this, although my eyes were open. What I saw was the lifeless corpses of the two men and the body that had formerly belonged to Julia suddenly fall to the ground with sickening thuds. Those who understand

They hung there in mid-air, miraculously suspended, … slowly twisting and turning …

such matters can claim that the souls of the three victims were "devoured" by Kamog, who, satisfied, then disappeared, returning from whence he came. The yawning breach in the heavens shriveled to nothingness and the blazing star diminished in luster until it blended into a sea of regular stars, one among countless others that the astronomers argue were the only heavenly bodies visible that night.

The aftermath was characterized by chaos and selfishness. The crowd immediately scattered in all directions, every man and woman caring only for themselves. Even those braggarts who claimed to be fearless in the face of Evil, the black-clad occultists, fled the graveyard in panic.

Only the two of us remained: I, and Julia, trapped in Rebecca's ruined cadaver. She had collapsed in the shadows during Kamog's manifestation. I walked over to see if there was any chance of reviving her, but then I noticed a twitching and trembling in the fallen body from which Rebecca's poor soul had just been extracted. That body was not dead, unlike its unfortunate male companions. It still breathed, and now it moved a little, partly raising itself up off the ground on unsteady arms. Julia's animated body lifted its head and stared at me. There was life in the eyes, the undeniable presence of a spirit, and a voice came from it that was not Rebecca's.

"Richard!" she gasped. "I'm back from the dead! Thank God, I'm alive!"

I could not answer her, so filled was I with joy and sympathy for my poor, long-suffering friend, the humble homeless poet, Miss Julia Spencer of Arkham.

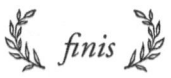 *finis*

About the Authors

DAVID BARKER has been writing supernatural fiction and poetry since the mid-1980s. In collaboration with the late W. H. Pugmire, he wrote three books of Lovecraftian fiction: *The Revenant of Rebecca Pascal* (Dark Renaissance Books, 2014), *In the Gulfs of Dream & Other Lovecraftian Tales* (Dark Renaissance Books, 2015) and *Witches in Dreamland* (Hippocampus Press, 2018), all three of which will be published in German language editions by Bärenklau Exklusiv. David's work has appeared in many magazines and anthologies including *Fungi, Cyäegha, Weird Fiction Review, The Audient Void, Nightmare's Realm, Forbidden Knowledge, Spectral Realms,* and *The Art Mephitic.* In 2020 his short story "Who Maketh Fertile the Fields" appeared in *A Walk in a Darker Wood: An Anthology of Folk Horror.* He lives in Oregon with his wife, Judy. They have four daughters.

WILUM HOPFROG PUGMIRE (W. H. Pugmire; 1951–2019) often described himself as "an obsessed Lovecraft fanboy" who wrote book after book of fiction in the Lovecraft tradition. Widely regarded as a master of weird fiction, his writing is notable for a richly poetical prose style and lush sensuality. The last single author collection published during his lifetime was *Monstrous Aftermath: Stories in the Lovecraftian Tradition* (Hippocampus Press, 2015). Posthumously released collections are *An Ecstasy of Fear* (Centipede Press, 2019) and *An Imp of Aether* (Hippocampus Press, 2019). His works are in various stages of being translated into German, Spanish, and Russian editions.

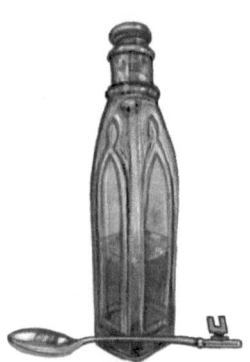

About the Artist

ERIN WELLS grew up on a farm in Southwestern Wisconsin. She earned a BA degree from Coe College in Cedar Rapids, Iowa, and an MFA from the Academy of Art University in San Francisco, California. She currently lives happily with her husband, Michael, amongst the redwoods in California's Santa Cruz Mountains, working as an illustrator and fine artist. She's created artwork for books by Scott Thomas, Gene O'Neill, Stephen King, Greg Gifune, Brett McBean, and others.

Colophon

The text was set in ADOBE GARAMOND.
Charcuterie was used for titling, ornaments,
and drop caps.